George Manville Fenn

The Parson O' Dumford

Vol. 1

George Manville Fenn

The Parson O' Dumford
Vol. 1

ISBN/EAN: 9783337342647

Printed in Europe, USA, Canada, Australia, Japan

Cover: Foto ©Andreas Hilbeck / pixelio.de

More available books at **www.hansebooks.com**

THE
PARSON O' DUMFORD.

A Tale.

BY

GEORGE MANVILLE FENN.

IN THREE VOLUMES.—VOL. I.

LONDON:
CHAPMAN AND HALL, 193 PICCADILLY.
1879.

CONTENTS OF VOL. I.

———○———

CONTENTS.

PARSON O' DUMFORD.

CHAPTER I.

PLEASANT RECEPTIONS.

" Ax."

" I was asking, or axing, as you call it, my man. I said, Is that Dumford, down there in the valley ? "

" And I said ax, or arks, as you call it, my man," was the surly, defiant reply.

The last speaker looked up savagely from the block of stone on which he was seated, and the questioner looked down from where he stood on the rough track. There was a quiet, half-amused twinkle in his clear grey eyes, which did not quit his verbal opponent for an instant, as he remained gazing at him without speaking.

They were men of about the same age—
eight-and-twenty or thirty—the one evidently a
clergyman by his white tie, and the clerical cut
of his clothes, though there was an easy *degagé*
look in the soft felt hat cocked a little on one
side of his massive head—a head that seemed
naturally to demand short crisp curly brown
hair. The same free and easy air showed in
the voluminous wrinkles of his grey tweed
trousers; his thick square-toed rather dusty
boots; and his gloveless hands, which were
brown, thickly veined, and muscular. He had
a small leather bag in one hand, a stout stick
in the other, and it was evident that he had
walked some distance over the hills, for the
nearest town, in the direction he had come,
was at least six miles away.

The seated man, who was smoking a very
dirty and short clay pipe, was as broad-
shouldered, as sturdy, and as well-knit; but
while the one, in spite of a somewhat heavy
build, was, so to speak, polished by exercise

into grace ; the other was rough and angular, and smirched as his countenance was by sweat and the grime of some manufacturing trade, he looked as brutal as his words.

"What are yow lookin' at ?" he suddenly growled menacingly.

"At yow," said the clergyman, in the most unruffled way ; and, letting his bag and stick fall in the ferns, he coolly seated himself on a second block of stone on the bright hill-side.

"Now look here," exclaimed the workman, roughly, "I know what you're after. You're going to call me my friend, and finish off with giving me a track, and you may just save yer- self the trouble, for it wean't do."

He knocked the ashes out of his pipe as he spoke, and looked menacing enough to do any amount of mischief to a man he did not like.

"You're wrong," said the traveller, coolly, as he rummaged in the pocket of his long black coat. " I'm going to have a pipe."

He opened a case, took out a well-blackened

meerschaum, scraped the ashes from its interior, filled it from a large india-rubber pouch which he then passed to the workman, before striking a match from a little brass box and beginning to smoke with his hands clasped round his knees.

" Try that tobacco," he continued. " You'll like it."

The workman took the tobacco-pouch in an ill-used way, stared at it, stared at the stranger smoking so contentedly by him, frowned, muttered something uncommonly like an oath, and ended by beginning to fill his pipe.

" Don't swear," said the traveller, taking his pipe from his lips for a moment, but only to replace it, and puff away like a practised smoker.

" Shall if I like," said the other, savagely. " What have yow got to do wi' it ?"

"Don't," said the traveller ; "what's the good ? It's weak and stupid. If you don't like a man, hit him. Don't swear."

The workman stared as these strange doctrines were enunciated ; then, after a moment's
hesitation, he finished filling his pipe, struck a
match which refused to light, threw it down
impatiently, tried another, and another, and
another, with the same result, and then uttered
a savage oath.

"At it again," said the traveller, coolly,
thrusting a hand into his pocket. " Why,
what a dirty-mouthed fellow you are."

" Yow wean't be happy till I've made your
mouth dirty," said the workman, savagely ;
" and you're going the gainest way to get it."

" Nonsense !" said the traveller, coolly.
" Why didn't you ask me for a light ?"

He handed his box of vesuvians, and it was
taken in a snatchy way. One was lighted, and
the few puffs of smoke which followed seemed
to have a mollifying effect on the smoker, who
confined himself to knitting his brows and
staring hard at the stranger, who now took off
his hat to let the fresh soft breeze blow over

his hot forehead, while he gazed down at the little town, with its square-towered church nestling amidst a clump of elms, beyond which showed a great blank, many-windowed building, with tall chimney shafts, two or three of which were vomiting clouds of black smoke nowise to the advantage of the landscape.

"I thowt you was a parson," said the young workman at last, in a growl a trifle less surly.

"Eh?" said the other, starting from a reverie, "parson? Yes, to be sure I am."

"Methody?"

"No."

"Ranter, p'r'aps?"

"Oh, no, only when I get a little warm."

"What are you, then?"

"Well, first of all," said the traveller, quietly, "you'd better answer my question. Is that Dumford?"

The workman hesitated and frowned. It seemed like giving in—being defeated—to answer now, but the clear grey eyes were fixed upon him in a way that seemed to influence his very being, and he said at last, gruffly,

"Well, yes, it is Doomford; and what if it is?"

"Oh, only that I'm the new vicar."

The workman puffed rapidly at his pipe, his face assuming a look of dislike, and at last he ejaculated,

"Ho!"

"Like that tobacco?" said the new vicar, quietly.

There was a pause, during which the workman seemed to be debating within himself whether he should answer or not. At last he condescended to reply,

"'Tain't bad."

"No; it's really good. I always get the best."

The last speaker took in at a glance what was going on in his companion's breast, and that was a fight between independent defiance and curiosity, but he seemed not to notice it.

"Give him time," he said to himself; and he smoked on, amused at the fellow's rough independence. He had been told that he would find Dumford a strange place, with a rough set of people; but nothing daunted, he had accepted the living, and had made up his mind how to act. At last the workman spoke:

"I never see a parson smoke afore!"

"Didn't you? Oh, I like a pipe."

"Ain't it wicked?" said the other, with a grin.

"Wicked? Why should it be? I see nothing wrong in it, or I should not do it."

There was another pause, during which pipes were refilled and lighted once more.

"Ever drink beer?" said the workman at last.

"Beer? By Samson!" exclaimed the new vicar, "how I should like a good draught now, my man. I'm very thirsty."

"Then there ain't none nigher than the Bull,

an' that's two mile away. There's plenty o'
watter."

" Where ? "

" Round the corner in the beck."

A short nod accompanied this, and the vicar
rose.

" Then we'll have a drop of water—qualified,"
he said, taking a flask from his pocket. " Scotch
whisky," he added, as he saw the stare directed
at the little flask, whose top he was unscrewing.

A dozen paces down the path, hidden by
some rocks, ran the source of a tiny rivulet or
beck, with water like crystal, and filling the
cup he took from his flask, the vicar qualified
it with whisky, handed it to his rough companion, and then drank a draught himself with
a sigh of relief.

" I've walked across the hills from Churley,"
he said, as they re-seated themselves. " I
wanted to see what the country was like."

" Ho ! " said the workman. " Say, you ain't
like the owd parson."

"I suppose not. Did you know him?"

"Know him? Not I. He warn't our sort."

"You used to go and hear him, I suppose?"

"Go and hear him? Well, that's a good one," said the workman; and a laugh transformed his face, driving away the sour, puckered look, which, however, began rapidly to return.

"What's the matter?" said the vicar, after a few minutes' silent smoking.

"Matter? matter wi' who?"

"Why, with you. What have you come up here for, all by yourself?"

"Nothing," was the reply, in the surliest of voices.

"Nonsense, man! Do you think I can't tell that you're put out—hipped—and that something has annoyed you?"

The young man's face gave a twitch or two, and he shuffled half round in his seat. Then, leaping up, he began to hurry off.

The new vicar had caught him in a dozen strides, putting away his pipe as he walked.

"There," he said, "I won't ask any more questions about yourself. I'm going down into the town, and we may as well walk together."

The young workman turned round to face him, angrily, but the calm unruffled look of his superior disarmed him, and he gave a bit of a gulp and walked on.

"I never quarrel with a man for being cross when he has had something to put him out," said the vicar, quietly. Then seeing that he was touching dangerous ground, he added, "By the way, where's the vicarage?"

"That's it, next the church," was the reply.

"Yes, I see; and what's that big building with the smoking chimneys?"

"Foundry," was said gruffly.

"To be sure, yes. Bell-foundry, isn't it?"

"Yes." Then after a pause, "I work theer."

"Indeed?"

"Tell you what," said the young man,

growing sociable in spite of himself; "yow get leave and I'll show you all about the works. No I wean't, though," he exclaimed, abruptly. "Cuss the works, I'll never go there no more."

The new vicar looked at him, tightening his lips a little.

"Another sore place, eh?" he said to himself, and turned the conversation once more.

"What sort of people are you at Dumford, my lad?"

"Hey? what sort o' people? Why, men and women and bairns, of course. What did you expect they weer?"

"I mean as to conduct," said the vicar, laughing. "What will they say to me, for instance?"

The young man's face grew less cloudy for a few moments, a broad, hearty, honest grin extending it so that he looked a frank, even handsome young fellow.

"They'll make it a bit warm for you, parson," he said at last.

"Eh? will they?" said the vicar, smiling. "Rough as you were, eh?"

"Oh no," said the other, quickly. "Don't you take no notice o' that. I ain't always that how. I was a bit popped this morning."

"Yes, I could see you were a bit *popped*," said the vicar. "We all have our troubles, my lad; but it's your true man that gets the strong hand of his anger and masters it."

"You look as if you never had nought to make you waxy in your life," said the workman. "I say, what do they call you?"

"Call me? A parson, I suppose."

"No; I mean call you. What's your name?"

"Oh! Selwood—Murray Selwood."

"Murray Selwood," said the questioner, repeating it to himself. "It's a curus sort o' name. Why didn't they call you Tom, or Harry, or Sam when thou wast a bairn?"

"Can't say," said the vicar, smiling. "I was too young to have a voice in the matter."

"You couldn't help it, of course. Say, can yow play cricket?"

"Oh yes."

"Bowl a bit, I suppose?"

"Yes; I'm best with the ball."

"Round hand?"

"Yes, and pretty sharp."

"Give's yer hand, parson, I like yow, hang me if I don't; and I'll come and hear you fust Sunday as you preaches."

The two men joined hands, and the grasp was long, earnest, and friendly, for the Reverend Murray Selwood, coming down freshly to his new living amongst people who had been described to him as little better than savages, felt that he had won one rough heart to his side, and was gladdened by the frank open gaze that met his own.

It was a different man that walked on now by his side, talking freely, in the rough independent way of the natives of his part; people who never thought of saying *Sir*, or touching their hat to any man—save and excepting the tradespeople, who contrived a salute to the wealthier families or clergy of the neighbourhood. He laughed as he talked of the peculiarities of Jacky this or Sammy that, and was in the midst of a speech about how parson would find " some of 'em rough 'uns to deal wi'," when he stopped short, set his teeth, drew in a long breath, and was in an instant an altered man.

The Reverend Murray Selwood saw and interpreted the change in a moment.

" Oh, 'tis love, 'tis love, 'tis love that makes the world go round," he said to himself; and he looked curiously at the little group upon which they had suddenly come on turning round by a group of weather-beaten, grey-lichened rocks.

There were two girls, one of whom was more than ankle-deep in a soft patch of bog, while the other was trying very hard to reach her and relieve her from her unpleasant predicament.

Danger there was none : a good wetting from
the amber-hued bog water being all that need
be feared ; but as the corner by the rocks was
turned it was evident that the spongy bog was
now rapidly giving way, and if help were to
be afforded it must be at once.

The young workman hesitated for a moment,
and then half turned away his head, but the
vicar ran forward as the maiden in distress
cried sharply—

"Oh Daisy, Daisy, what shall I do ?"

"Let me help you out," said the vicar,
smiling. "Why, it is soft here," he cried, as
he went in over his knees, but got one foot on
a tuft of dry heath and dragged out the other,
to plant it upon a patch of grass. "Don't be
alarmed. There, both hands on my shoulder.
That's right. Hold tight, I've got you. Why
you were sinking fast, and planting yourself as
a new kind of marsh flower—and—there, don't
shrink away, or we shall be both planted—to
blossom side by side. It *is* soft—that's better

—now lean all your weight on me, my dear—
not that you're heavy—now I have you—
steady it is—that's better."

As he kept up this running fire of disconnected words, he contrived to drag the girl out
of the soft bog, placing his arm well round her
waist, and then carried her in his arms, stepping
cautiously from tussock to tussock till he placed
her blushing and trembling beside her companion, who had retreated to the firm ground.

" Oh, thank you. I am so much obliged,"
stammered the girl, as her long lashes were
lowered over her pretty hazel eyes, which
shrank from the honest admiring gaze directed
upon them.

And truly there was something to admire in
the pretty, innocent, girlish face with its
creamy complexion, and wavy dark brown
hair, several little tresses of which had been
blown loose by the breeze on the hill-side.

She was very plainly dressed, and wore a
simple coarse straw hat, but there was an air

of refinement about her which, before she
opened her lips, told the new vicar that he
was in the presence of one who had been born
in a sphere of some culture.

Not so her companion, who, though as well
favoured by nature, was cast in quite another
mould.   Plump, peachy, and rounded of out-
line, she was a thorough specimen of the
better class English cottage girl, spoiled by her
parents, and imbued with a knowledge that she
was the pretty girl of the place.

" I am so much obliged—it was so good of
you," stammered the heroine of the bog.

" Not at all, my dear; don't mention it,"
said the vicar, in a quiet way that helped to
put the discomfited maiden at her ease.   " I
see : gathering bog-flowers and went too far.
For shame," he continued, loudly.   " You, a
country young lady, and not to know it was
dangerous to go where the cotton rushes grow.
You wanted some, eh ?   Yes, and left the
basket out there—half full."

"Oh, pray don't go—never mind the basket —it does not matter," faltered the girl; but the vicar was already stepping from tussock to tussock, ending by hooking up the basket with his stick, and pausing to pick some of the best silky topped rushes within his reach.

"There," he said, returning the basket and its contents; "there are your cotton rushes— earth's fruit. I ought to scold you for behaving like a daughter of Eve, and trying to get what you ought not to touch."

The girl crimsoned to the roots of her hair at the word Eve, and exchanged glances with her companion, who was standing before her, looking hot, frowning, and cross, with her eyes fixed on the ground, and her nose in the air, as if being scourged by the angry look directed at her by the young workman, who stood a few yards off scowling, with his hands thrust into the very bottoms of his pockets.

"I did not think the bog was so treacherous,"

said the girl, stealing a look at the frank, manly face before her. " It looked so safe."

" So do many things in this world, my dear; but you must not trust them any the more for their fair seeming."

The girl started a little, and looked indignant at the familiar way in which she was addressed by so young a man—a perfect stranger. She had already tried to sting him in the bog with two or three furious darts from her bright eyes for daring to put his arms round her. In fact she had felt for a moment that she would rather sink into the earth than be touched like that, but she was helpless and had to resign herself to her fate.

" Ah!" said the vicar, " you are looking angry at me for speaking in such a free way."

" I—I indeed—I——"

" Ah, my dear, I can read that pretty innocent face of yours like a book. There—there —don't blush so. We are strangers : well, let's be strangers no more. Let me introduce myself. I am Murray Selwood, your new parson, and you are——?"

"Eve Pelly—Mrs. Glaire's——"

"Niece. I know, my dear. Very, very glad to make your acquaintance. You see I know something about the place, though I have not been there yet."

As he spoke he took the timidly extended hand and gave it a warm, frank pressure, which again heightened the blush; but in a few moments Eve Pelly felt more at her ease in the presence of this stranger, who, with all his freedom, had an atmosphere of gentlemanly truth and candour which won upon all with whom he came in contact.

"Now," he said, "you must introduce me to my other little friend here. Who is this?"

"This is Daisy Banks, Mr. Selwood. Mr. Banks is my aunt's foreman at the Foundry. Daisy comes with me sometimes when I go for a walk. We have known each other from children."

"To be sure," said the vicar, smiling. "I might have known your name was Daisy. Shake hands, my dear. You'll never change that name, but some day you'll be coming to me to change the other for you."

"Which I'm sure I never shall," cried Daisy, with an indignant stamp, and a hot angry glance at the young workman, who ground his teeth, and savagely kicked the top off a tuft of heather.

"Don't be angry, my dear," said the vicar, kindly, as, red-faced, choking, and hardly able to restrain her angry tears, the girl snatched away her hand and turned away.

"It's one of my weaknesses to touch tender chords unwittingly," he said in a low tone to Eve; and, how it was she knew not, the girl felt herself drawn into a feeling of confidence with this stranger, who, however, half affronted her susceptibilities the next moment by saying,

"But come, you must not stand here with

wet feet. If you were a sister of mine I should make you take off those dripping boots."

"They are not wet—not very wet," she stammered, correcting herself.

"I think I know," said the vicar, smiling. "But come, you must walk home sharply. I'm a bit of a doctor in my way. You won't mind my company, I hope. We must be very good friends."

"I'm sure we shall," said Eve, frankly, as she glanced once more at her companion, and the next minute he was chatting to her about the contents of her basket.

"Then you understand botany?" she said, eagerly, and he looked down with pleasure at the bright, animated countenance at his side.

"Oh, yes, a little. And you do, I see?"

"Oh, a very little," said Eve; "the hard Latin words are so puzzling."

"But you can learn plenty of botany without troubling yourself over the long names; they will come to you imperceptibly."

Meanwhile Daisy, who had been forgotten, had followed on a few yards behind, looking very angry and indignant at the way in which she was neglected, while the young workman walking by her side seemed as angry, but with a dash of the savage in his face.

Both looked straight before them, and neither spoke, each going on as if in utter ignorance of the companion's presence.

"I shall have to give you some lessons when I begin making my collection of specimens," said the vicar, after a few more observations.

"Will you?" exclaimed Eve, eagerly; and then, recalling the fact that she had known this stranger but a few minutes, she tried to qualify her remark, failed dismally, and began to feel exceedingly hot and conscious, when there was a diversion.

They had been gradually nearing the town, and had reached a spot where the moorland gave place to cultivated soil, when a young man, dressed in a rather fast style, and with a cigar in his mouth, suddenly leaped over a stile, and started and looked quite awkward on finding himself face to face with this group.

He was a slight fair young fellow, of some four-and-twenty, with rather pale downy whiskers, and a blonde silky moustache, which was carefully waxed into points. His dress was a light tweed suit, but to condone for the sombre hue of it and his grey deerstalker hat, he wore a brilliant scarlet tie slipped through a massive gold ring, and wore several rings on his thin effeminate fingers.

The effect upon the party caused by the sudden appearance of this personage was varied.

Daisy, who had resumed the natural tint of her complexion—a peachy hue touched rather warmly by the brown of the sun—became as though the new-comer's tie was reflected to her very temples; the young workman's face grew black as night, and his teeth grated together as his pockets suddenly bulged out, indicative of doubled fists, and he stared at the dandy in a menacing way that betokened evil.

As for Eve, she ran forward with a little joyous cry and took the young man's arm.

"Ah, Dick," she cried, "I didn't expect you. How kind of you to come."

"Didn't come to meet you," said the young man, shortly, as he fixed a glass with some difficulty in his eye to stare at the stranger.

"Then you ought to have come," said Eve, quickly. "Take that stupid glass out of your eye, you silly boy," she whispered. Then aloud, "I've been in such trouble, Dick, dear."

"Dick, dear!" He did not know why it was, but this very familiar appellation from those soft red lips seemed to jar on the stranger's ears, and he drew a longer breath than usual.

"I actually got bogged, Dick, and was sinking, when this gentleman came and saved me. Dick, dear, this is our new vicar. Mr.

Selwood, this is Mr. Richard Glaire of the Foundry."

"Glad to know you, Mr. Glaire," said the vicar, holding out his hand.

"How do?" said the new-comer, shortly, and his hand went out in a slow, awkward, unwilling way, retiring afterwards from the hearty grasp it received in a very sharp manner, for thin effeminate hands, that do not return an honest pressure, fare badly in a manly grasp, especially if they happen to be half-covered with unnecessary rings.

"How do? Glad to see you," said the young owner of the Foundry, though it was always more looked upon since his father's death as the property of Mrs. Glaire. "Find this rather dull place."

"I don't think I shall," said the vicar, looking at him curiously.

"Very dull place," said the young man. "Very. Come, Evey. You'll call, I suppose?"

"Of course I shall," said the vicar, smiling. "I mean to know everybody here."

"Thanks, much," said Mr. Glaire, glancing at Daisy, who gave herself an angry twitch and turned away. He then drew Eve's arm through his own, and, raising his hat slightly to the vicar, was turning away when his eye lit on the young workman. "Hallo you, Tom Podmore," he cried, "how is it you're not at work?"

"That's my business," growled the man. "I'll tell you that when you ain't got young missus there wi' you, and I wean't afore."

Richard Glaire looked at the sturdy fellow uneasily, and directed a second glance at Daisy, his vacillating eyes resting for a moment on the pocketed double fists before repeating his words shortly—

"Come along, Evey."

"Wait a moment, Dick, dear," she said, disengaging her arm. "How rude you are!" she added in an undertone. "Good day, Mr.

Selwood, and thank you very much," she said,
ingenuously. "Pray come and see us soon.
Aunt will be so glad to know you. She was
talking about you last night, and wondering
what you would be like. Good-bye."

She held out her hand, and the constraint
that was in spite of himself creeping over the
new vicar was thawed away by the genial,
innocent sunshine of the young girl's smile.

"Good-bye," he said, frankly ; and his face
lit up with pleasure. "I shall call very soon,
and we won't forget the botany."

"Oh, no," said Eve, as her arm was once
more pinioned. "Come, Daisy, you are coming
up to the house."

"No, thank you, miss; I must go home
now."

As she spoke she hurried forward, tripped
over the stile first, and was gone.

A minute later and Eve had lightly touched
Richard Glaire's arm, and climbed the stile in
her turn, leaving the vicar to follow slowly,

forgetful of the presence of the young workman
—Podmore.

He was brought back from his dreamy
musings on the relation existing between the
young fellow who had just gone, and the sweet
innocent girl who was his companion, by a
rough grasp being laid upon his arm, and
turning sharply, there stood Tom Podmore,
with the veins in his forehead swelling, and
his face black with rage.

CHAPTER II.

TOM PODMORE'S GRIEVANCE.

" LOOK here, parson," cried the young workman, in a voice husky with emotion; and as
he spoke he dashed his cap upon the ground
and began to roll up his sleeves, displaying
arms fit, with their sturdy rolls of muscle, for a
young Hercules. " Look here, parson. You're
a straanger here, and I'll tell 'ee. That's my
master, that is, and I shall kill him afore I've
done."

" Hush, man, hush!" cried the young vicar.

"I don't keer, I shall. Why ain't I at
work, eh? Never another stroke will I do for
him; wish that my hammer may come on my
head if I do. Look here, parson," he went on,
catching the other's arm hard in a grasp of

iron, "that's his lass, that is—that's his young lady—Miss Eve Pelly ; God bless her for a perfect angel, and too good for him. He's engaged to her, he is—engaged to be married, and he's got thousands and thousands of his own, and the Foundry, and horses to hunt wi', and he ain't satisfied. No, no ; I ain't done yet. Look here, ain't all that enough for any man ? You know what's right, and what ain't. What call's he got to come between me and she ? "

He jerked one fist in the direction taken by Daisy, and went on.

" Things ran all right between us before he steps in with his London dandy air, and his short coot hair, and fine clothes. Old Joe Banks was willing ; and as for Missus Banks, why, bless her, she's always been like a mother to me. I'd saved up a hundred and sixty pun' ten, all hard earnings, and we was soon to be married, and then he comes between us and turns the girl's head. You come on to me

when I'd gone up the hill-side there, to chew
it all over, after she'd huffed me this morning,
and I coot up rough. I say, warn't it enough to
make any man coot up rough?"

"It was, indeed, Podmore," said the vicar,
kindly.

"But I wean't stand it, that I wean't," roared
the young man, like an angry bull. "A man's
a man even if he is a master. I'll fight fair;
but if I don't break every bone in his false
skin, my name ain't Tom Podmore."

This burst over, he resumed his cap and
snatched down his sleeves, looking half ashamed
of his effusion in the presence of a stranger,
and he shrank away a little as the vicar laid
his hand upon his arm.

"Look here, Podmore," he said kindly;
"when I went first to school they used to give
me for a copy to write, 'Do nothing rashly.'
Don't you do anything rashly, my friend,
because things done in haste are repented of
at leisure. I have come down here to be a

friend, I hope, to everybody, and as you were the first man I met in Dumford, I shall look upon you as one of the first to have a call upon me."

"Thanky, sir, thanky kindly," said Podmore, in a quieter tone. "I don't know how it is, but you've got a kind of way with you that gets over a fellow."

"She seems a nice, pretty, well-behaved girl, that Daisy Banks," said the vicar.

"There isn't a better nor a truer-hearted girl nor a prettier nowhere for twenty miles round," cried the young fellow, flushing up with a lover's pride. "Why look at her, sir, side by side with Miss Eve, that's a born lady. Why, Miss Eve's that delicate and poor beside my Daisy, as there ain't no comparison 'tween 'em. My Daisy, as was," he added, sorrowfully. "Something's come over her like of late, and it's all over now."

The great strong fellow turned his back, and resting one hand upon the stile, his broad shoulders gave a heave or two.

"I shan't take on about it," he said, roughly, as he turned round with a sharp, defiant air of recklessness. "I ain't the first fool that's been jilted by a woman. Say, parson—hundred and sixty pound 'll buy a sight o' gills o' ale. Don't you take no heed o' what I said."

He was turning away, but a strong hand was upon his shoulder.

"Look here, Podmore," said the vicar, firmly, "you said something about fools just now. You are not a fool, and you know it. You leave the ale alone—to the fools—and go back and get to work as hard, or harder, than you ever worked before. I shall see you again soon, perhaps bowl to you in the cricket field. As for your affairs, you leave them to me. Do you know why Englishmen make the best soldiers?"

"Do I know why Englishmen make the best soldiers, parson?" said Podmore, staring. "No: can't say I do."

"Because, my lad, they never know when

they are beaten. Now, you are not beaten yet.
Good-bye."

He held out his hand, and the great grimy,
horny palm of the workman came down into
it with a loud clap, and the grip that ensued
from each side would have been unpleasant to
any walnut between their palms.

Then they parted, taking different routes, and
ten minutes later the Reverend Murray Selwood
was walking quietly through the empty town
street, quite conscious though that head after
head was being thrust out to have a look at
the stranger.

There was the usual sprinkling of shops and
private houses, great blank red-brick dwellings,
which told their own tale of being the houses
of the lawyer, the doctor, and their newer
opponents. Then there was the factory-look-
ing place, with great gates to the yard, and a
time-keeper's lodge inside, surmounted by a
bell in its little wooden hutch. The throb of
machinery could be heard, and the shriek of

metal being tortured into civilized form came painfully to the ear from time to time. Smoke hung heavily in the air—smoke tinged with lurid flame; and above all came the roar of the reverberating furnaces, where steel or some alloy was being fused for the castings which had made out-of-the-way, half-savage Dumford, with its uncouth, independent people, famous throughout the length and breadth of the land.

There were very few people visible, for the works had not yet begun to pour forth their masses of working bees, but there were plenty of big rough lads hanging about the corners of the streets.

"I wonder what sort of order the schools are in," said the new vicar to himself, as he neared the church, towards which he was bending his steps, meaning to glance round before entering the vicarage. "Yes, I wonder what sort of a condition they are in. Bad, I fear. Very bad, I'm sure," he added.

For at that moment a great lump of furnace refuse, or glass, there known as slag, struck him a heavy blow in the back.

He turned sharply, but not a soul was visible, and he stooped and picked up the lump, which was nearly equal in size to his fist.

"Yes, no doubt about it, very bad," he said. "Well, I'll take you to my new home, and you shall have the first position in my cabinet of specimens, being kept as a memorial of my welcome to Dumford."

"Well," he said, as he reached the church gate, "I've made two friends already, and—perhaps—an enemy. By Jove, there's another brick."

CHAPTER III.

AT THE FOUNDRY HOUSE.

MRS. GLAIRE lived in a great blank-looking red-brick house in the main street, two ugly steep stone steps coming down from the front door on to the narrow kidney pebble path, and encroaching so upon the way that they were known as the tipsy-turvies, in consequence of the number of excited Dumfordites who fell over them in the dark. Though for the matter of that they were awkward for the most sober wayfarer, and in a town with a Local Board would have been condemned long before.

The ugliness of the Foundry House, as it was called, only dwelt on the side giving on the street; the back opened upon an extensive garden, enclosed by mighty red-brick walls, for the greater part concealed by the dense foliage, which made the fine old garden a bosky wilderness of shady lawn, walk, and shrubbery.

For Mrs. Glaire was great upon flowers, in fact, after "my son, Richard," her garden stood at the top of her affections, even before her niece, Eve, whom she loved very dearly all the same.

Mrs. Glaire was a little busy ant of a woman, with a pleasant, fair face, ornamented with two tufts of little fuzzy blonde curls, which ought to have hung down, but which seemed to be screwed up so tightly that they took delight in sticking out at all kinds of angles, one or two of the most wanton—those with the rough ends—that had been untwisted by Mrs. Glaire's curl-papers, even going so far as to stick straight up.

On the morning when the new vicar made his entry into Dumford, Mrs. Glaire was out in her garden busy. She had on her brown holland apron, and her print drawn hood, the strings of which seemed to cut deeply into her little double chin, and altogether did nothing to improve her personal appearance. A little basket was in one hand half-filled with the dead leaves of geraniums which she had been snipping off with the large garden scissors she held in the other hand—scissors which, for fear of being mislaid, were attached to a silken cord, evidently the former trimming of some article of feminine attire, and this cord was tied round her waist.

She had two attendants—Prince and the gardener, Jacky Budd—Jacky: for it was the peculiarity of Dumford that everybody was known by a familiar interpretation of his Christian name, or else by a *sobriquet* more quaint than pleasant.

Prince was a King Charles spaniel, with the shortest of snub noses, the most protrusive of great intelligent eyes, and long silky ears that nearly swept the ground. Prince had a weakness, and that was fat. He had been fed into such a state of rotundity that he had long ceased running and barking, even at cats, against which he was supposed to have a wonderful antipathy, and he passed his time after his regular meals in sleeping, when he was lying down, and wheezing when he was standing up, and never if he could possibly help it did he move from the position in which he was placed.

Jacky Budd, the gardener, was a pale, sodden-looking man, the only tinge of colour in his countenance being in his nose, and that tinge was given by a few fiery veins. He had a knack when addressed of standing with one thumb stuck in the arm-hole of his ragged vest, which was stretched and worn in consequence, and this attitude was a favourite with him on Sundays, and was maintained just inside the south door till all the people were in church, when he went to his own sitting beneath the reading desk, for Jacky Budd, in addition to being a gardener, was the parish clerk.

Jacky had his weakness, like Prince, but it

was very different from that of the dog ; in fact, it was one that troubled a great many of the people of Dumford, who looked upon it with very lenient eyes. For though the gentleman in question had been suspended by the late vicar for being intoxicated in church, and saying out loud in reading the psalms, " As it (hic) was in the beginning (hic) is now (hic) and ever shall be (hic)," he was penitent and forgiven at the end of the week, and he sinned no more until the next time.

The late vicar was compelled to take notice of the backsliding, even though people said he was troubled with the same weakness, for Miss Purley, the doctor's sister, burst out laughing quite loud in consequence of a look given her by Richard Glaire from the opposite pew. Her brother was there, and to pass it off he made a stir about it, and had her carried out, to come back after a few minutes on tip-toe and whisper to two or three people that it was a touch of hysterics.

Those who knew Jacky could tell when he had been drinking from the stolid look upon his countenance, and Mrs. Glaire was one of those who knew him.

"Come along, Prince," she cried in a shrill chirpy treble, and stooping down she lifted and carried Prince a few yards, to set him down beside a rustic flower-stand, rubbing his leg with the rim of the basket, and Prince went on wheezing, while his mistress began to snip.

Jacky followed slowly with a pot of water, a fluid that he held in detestation, and considered to be only useful for watering flowers.

"Now, Jacky," exclaimed his mistress, "these pots are quite dry. Give them all some water."

"Yes, mum," said Jacky; and raising the pot, he began with trembling hands to direct erratic streams amongst the flowers, then shaking his head, stopping, and examining the spout as if that were in fault.

"Stone got in it, I think," he muttered.

"You've been drinking again, Jacky," exclaimed his mistress, shaking the scissors at him threateningly.

"Drinking, mum! drinking!"

This in a tone of injured surprise.

"Yes, you stupid man. Do you think I don't know? I can smell you."

"Drinking!" said Jacky, putting his hand to his head, as if to collect his thoughts. "Yes, so I did; I had a gill of ale last night."

"Now, Jacky, I won't have it," exclaimed Mrs. Glaire. "If you try to deceive me I won't keep you on."

"What, and turn away a faithful servant as made this garden what it is, mum, and nursed Master Dick when he was a bit of a bairn no bigger than——"

Jacky stooped down to try and show how many inches high Dick Glaire was when his nursing days were on; and as the gardener placed his hand horizontally, it seemed that about six inches must have been the stature of the child. But this was a dangerous experiment, and Jacky nearly overbalanced himself. A sharp question from his mistress, however, brought him upright, and somewhat sobered him.

"Have you heard any more about that, Jacky?"

"'Bout Master Richard, mum?"

"Yes, Jacky. But mind this, I hate talebearing and the gossip of the place."

"You do, mum; you allus did," said Jacky, winking solemnly to himself; "but that's a fact."

"I won't believe it, Jacky," said Mrs. Glaire, snipping off sound leaves and blossoms in her agitation.

"It's a fact, mum, and I don't wonder at your feeling popped."

"I'm not cross at all, Jacky," exclaimed Mrs. Glaire, with her face working, "for I don't believe my son would stoop in that way."

"But it's a fack, mum; and you must send him away, or he'll be taking a wife from among the Midianitish women. That's so."

"Now, I don't want to hear gossip, man; but what have you heard? There, do stand still or you'll tread on Prince."

"Heard, mum? Lots. You should say, 'What have you seen?'"

"Seen! Have you seen anything?"

Jacky put his thumb very far into his arm-hole, and spread his fingers very wide, as he rolled his head solemnly.

"You won't tell Master Richard as you heard of it from me, mum?"

"No, Jacky, no; certainly not."

"And get me kicked out without a moment's notice?"

"No, no, certainly not. Now tell me directly."

"Well, mum, Missus Hubley says as she knows he's always arter her."

"What, Daisy Banks?"

Jacky nodded.

" But she's a mischief-making, gossiping old —woman ! " exclaimed Mrs. Glaire ; " and her word isn't worth anything.   You said you had seen something."

Jacky nodded, and screwed up his face as he laid his finger beside his nose.

" If you don't speak directly, man, I shall do you a mischief," exclaimed the little woman, excitedly.   " Tell me all you know this instant."

" Well, you see, mum, it was like this : last night was very dark, and my missus said to me, ' Jacky,' she says, ' take the boocket and go down to Brown's poomp and get a boocket o' watter.'   Because you see, mum, the sucker being wore, our poomp's not agate just now."

" Well ! " exclaimed Mrs. Glaire, impatiently.

" Well, mum, I goes round by Kitty Rawson's corner, and out back way, and I come upon Master Richard wi' his arm round Daisy Banks's waist."

"Now, Jacky," exclaimed Mrs. Glaire, with a hysterical sob, "if this is not the truth I'll never, never forgive you."

"Truth, mum," said Jacky, in an ill-used tone. "I've been clerk here a matter o' twenty year, and my father and grandfather before me, and would I tell a lie, do you think? Speak the truth without fear or favour. Amen."

"Go away now," cried Mrs. Glaire, sharply.

"Wean't I water all the plants, mum?"

"No; go away, and if you say a word to a soul about this, I'll never forgive you, Jacky, never."

"Thanky, mum, thanky," said Jacky, turning to go, and nearly trampling on Prince.

"No, come here!" exclaimed Mrs. Glaire, whose face was working. "Go round to the foundry, and tell Joe Banks I want to speak to him. Tell him I'm in the garden."

"Yes, mum."

"Jacky," she said, calling him back.

" Yes, mum."

"Don't you dare to say a word about what it's for."

" No, mum."

Jacky went off round by his tool-shed, out into the street, and down to the foundry gates, where, after a word with the gateman, he went on across the great metal-strewn yard in search of Mrs. Glaire's sturdy foreman.

Meanwhile that lady caught up her dog, and carried him to a garden seat, where, upon being set down, he curled up and went to sleep, his tail and ears combined, making a comfortable coverlid. Then taking off her scissors and placing them in her basket, Mrs. Glaire seated herself, sighing deeply, and taking out from a voluminous pocket, which took sundry evolutions with drapery to reach, a great ball of lambswool and a couple of knitting pins, she began to knit rapidly what was intended to be some kind of undergarment for her only son.

"Oh, Dick, Dick," she muttered; "you'll break my heart before you've done."

The knitting pins clicked loudly, and a couple of bright tears stole down her cheeks and dropped into her lap.

"And I did not tell him to hold his tongue before Eve," she exclaimed, sharply. "Tut-tut —tut—tut! This must be stopped; this must be stopped."

The sighing, lamenting phase gave place by degrees to an angry one. The pins clicked sharply, and the pleasant grey head was perked, while the lips were tightened together even as were the stitches in the knitting, which had to be all undone.

Just then the garden door opened, and a broad-shouldered grizzled man of seven or eight and forty entered the garden followed by Jacky. Foreman though he was, Joe Banks had been hard at work, and his hands and face bore the grime of the foundry. He had, however, thrown on a jacket, and wiped the perspiration from his forehead, leaving a half clean line over his pale blue eyes, while a pleasant smile puckered such of his face as was not hidden by his closely cut grizzled beard.

"Sarvant, ma'am," he said, making a rough bow to the lady of the house.

"Good morning, Banks," said Mrs. Glaire. "Jacky, go and nail up that wistaria, and mind you don't tumble off the ladder."

Jacky looked injured, but walked off, evidently making a bee line for the tool-shed, one which he did not keep.

"Little on, mum," said the foreman, with a wise nod in Jacky's direction. "Wants a month's illness to be a warnin'."

"It's a pity, Banks, but he will drink."

"Like lots more on 'em, ma'am. Why if I was to get shut of all the lads in the works there who like their drop of drink, I shouldn't have half enew."

"How are things going on, Banks?" said Mrs. Glaire.

The foreman looked at her curiously, for it was a new thing for his mistress to make any inquiry about the foundry. A few months back and he had to make his daily reports, but since Richard Glaire had come of age, Mrs. Glaire had scrupulously avoided interfering in any way, handing over the business management to "my son."

"I said how are things going on in the foundry, Banks," said the lady again, for the foreman had coughed and shuffled from one foot on to the other.

"Do you wish me to tell you, ma'am?" he said at last.

"Tell me? of course," said Mrs. Glaire, impatiently. "How are matters?"

"Bad."

"Bad? What do you mean?"

"Well, mum, not bad as to work; 'cause there's plenty of that, and nothing in the way of contracts as is like to suffer by waiting."

"Then, what do you mean?"

"Well, you see, ma'am, Mr. Richard don't get on wi' the men. He wants to have it all his own way, and they want to have it all theirn. Well, of course that wean't work; so what's wanted is for the governor to give way just a little, and then they'd give way altogether."

"But I'm sure my son Richard's management is excellent," said Mrs. Glaire, whose lip quivered a little as she drew herself up with dignity, and began a fresh row of her knitting.

Banks coughed slightly, and remained silent.

"Don't you think so, Banks?"

"Well, you see, ma'am, he's a bit arbitrary."

"Arbitrary? What do you mean, Banks?"

"Well, you see, ma'am, he turned Sim Slee off at a moment's notice."

"And quite right, too," said Mrs. Glaire, hotly. "My son told me. The fellow is a spouting, mouthing creature."

"He is that, ma'am, and as lazy as a slug, but it made matters worse, and just now there's a deal of strikes about, and the men at other places listening to delegates from societies, and joining unions, and all that sort of stuff."

" And have you joined one of those clubs, Joe Banks?" said Mrs. Glaire, sharply.

" Me join 'em, ma'am ? Not I," said Banks, who seemed immensely tickled at the idea. " Not I. I'm foreman, and get my wage reg'lar, and I don't want none of their flummery. You should hear Ann go on about 'em."

" I beg your pardon, Banks," said Mrs. Glaire. " I might have known that you were too sensible a man to go to these meetings."

" Well, as to being sensible, I don't know about that, Missus Glaire. Them two women folk at home do about what they like wi' me."

" I don't believe it, Joe," said Mrs. Glaire. " Daisy would not have grown up such a good, sensible girl if she had not had a firm, kind, sensible father."

" God bless her!" said Joe, and a little moisture appeared in one eye. Then speaking

rather huskily—"Thank you, ma'am—thank
you, Missus Glaire. I try to do my duty by
her, and so does Ann."

"Is Ann quite well?"

"Quite well, thank you kindly, ma'am,"
said the foreman. "Don't you be afeared for me,
Missus Glaire. I worked with Richard Glaire,
senior, thirty years ago, two working lads,
and we was always best of friends both when
we was poor, and when I saw him gradually
grow rich, for he had a long head, had your
husband, while I'd only got a square one.
But I stuck to him, and he stuck to me, and
when he died, leaving me his foreman, you
know, Mrs. Glaire, how he sent for me, and
'Joe,' he says, 'good bye, God bless you!
You've always been my right hand man. Stick
to my son.'"

"He did, Joe, he did," said Mrs. Glaire, with
a deep sigh, and a couple of tears fell on her
knitting.

"And I'll stick to him through thick and

thin," said the foreman, stoutly. "For I never envied Dick, his father—there, 'tain't 'spectful to you, ma'am, to say Dick, though it comes natural — I never envied Master Glaire his success with his contracts, and getting on to be a big man. I was happy enough; but you know, ma'am, young Master Dick is arbitrary; he is indeed, and he can't feel for a working man like his father did."

"He is more strict you see, Banks, that is all," said Mrs. Glaire, stiffly; and the foreman screwed up his face a little.

"You advise him not to be quite so strict, ma'am. I wouldn't advise you wrong, as you know."

"I know that, Joe Banks," said Mrs. Glaire, smiling pleasantly; "and I'll say a word to him. But I wanted to say something to you."

"Well, I've been a wondering why you sent for me, ma'am," said the foreman, bluntly.

"You see," said Mrs. Glaire, hesitating, "there are little bits of petty tattle about."

"What, here, ma'am," said the foreman, with a hearty laugh. "Of course there is, and always was, and will be."

"But they are about Daisy," said Mrs. Glaire, dashing at last into the matter.

"I should just like to get hold of the man as said a word against my lass," said Banks, stretching out a tremendous fist. "I'd crack him, I would, like a nut. But what have they been saying?"

CHAPTER IV.

DAISY'S FATHER.

"WELL," said Mrs. Glaire, who found her task more difficult than she had apprehended, "the fact is, they say she has been seen talking to my son."

"Is that all?" said the foreman, laughing in a quiet, hearty way.

"Yes, that is all, and for Daisy's sake I want it stopped. Have you heard or known anything?"

"Well, to put it quite plain, the missus wants her to have Tom Podmore down at the works there, but the girl hangs back, and I found out the reason. I did see Master Dick talking to her one night, and it set me a thinking."

"And you didn't stop it?" exclaimed Mrs. Glaire, sharply.

"Stop it? Why should I stop it?" said the foreman. "She's getting on for twenty, and is sure to begin thinking about sweethearts. Ann did when she was nineteen, and if I recollect right, little fair-haired Lisbeth Ward was only eighteen when she used to blush on meeting Dick Glaire. I see her do it," said the bluff fellow, chuckling.

"But that was long ago," exclaimed Mrs. Glaire, excitedly. "Positions are changed since then. My son——"

"Well, ma'am, he's a workman's son, and my bairn's a workman's daughter. I've give her a good schooling, and she's as pretty a lass as there is in these parts, and if your son Richard's took a fancy to her, and asks me to let him marry her, and the lass likes him, why I shall say yes, like a man."

Mrs. Glaire looked at him aghast. This was a turn in affairs she had never anticipated, and one which called forth all her knowledge of human nature to combat.

"But," she exclaimed, "he is engaged to his cousin here, Miss Pelly."

"Don't seem like it," chuckled the foreman. "Why, he's always after Daisy now."

"Oh, this is dreadful!" gasped Mrs. Glaire, dropping her knitting. "I tell you he is engaged—promised to be married to his second cousin, Miss Pelly."

"Stuff!" said Banks, laughing. "He'll never marry she, though she's a good, sweet girl."

"Don't I tell you he will," gasped Mrs. Glaire. "Man, man, are you blind? This is dreadful to me, but I must speak. Has it never struck you that my son may have wrong motives with respect to your child?"

"What?" roared the foreman; and the veins in his forehead swelled out, as his fists clenched. "Bah!" he exclaimed, resuming his calmness. "Nonsense, ma'am, nonsense. What! Master Dicky Glaire, my true old friend's son, mean wrong by my lass Daisy? Mrs. Glaire, ma'am, Mrs. Glaire, for shame, for shame ! "

" The man's infatuated ! " exclaimed Mrs. Glaire, and she stared wonderingly at the bluff, honest fellow before her.

" Why, ma'am," said the foreman, smiling, " I wouldn't believe it of him if you swore it. He's arbitrary, and he's too fond of his horses, and dogs, and sporting : but my Daisy ! Oh, for shame, ma'am, for shame ! He loves the very ground on which she walks."

" And—and "—stammered Mrs. Glaire, " does —does Daisy care for him ? Fool that I was to let her come here and be so intimate with Eve," she muttered.

" Well, ma'am," said the foreman, thoughtfully, " I'm not so sure about that."

He was about to say more when Mrs. Glaire stopped him.

" Another time, Banks, another time," she said, hastily. " Here is my son."

As she spoke Richard Glaire came into the garden with his hands in his pockets, and Eve Pelly clinging to one arm, looking bright and happy.

The foreman started slightly, but gave himself a jerk and smiled, and then, in obedience to a gesture from his mistress, he left the garden and returned to the foundry.

CHAPTER V.

THE VICAR'S STROLL.

THE brick, as the vicar called it, was only another piece of slag; but he did not turn his head, only smiled, and began thinking that Dumford quite equalled the report he had heard of it. Then looking round the plain old church, peering inside through the windows, and satisfying himself that its architectural beauties were not of a very striking nature, he turned aside and entered the vicarage garden, giving a sigh of satisfaction on finding that his home was a comfortable red-brick, gable-ended house, whose exterior, with its garden overrun with weeds, promised well in its traces of former cultivation.

A ring at a bell by the side post of the

door brought forth a wan, washed-out looking woman, who looked at the visitor from top to toe, ending by saying sharply, in a vinegary tone of voice:

" What d'yer want ? "

" To come in," said the vicar, smiling. " Are you in charge of the house ? "

" If yow want to go over t'church yow must go to Jacky Budd's down street for the keys. I wean't leave place no more for nobody."

" But I don't want to go over the church— at least not now. I want to come in, and see about having a room or two made comfortable."

" Are yow t'new parson, then ? "

" Yes, I'm the new parson."

" Ho ! Then yow'd best come in."

The door was held open, and looking at him very suspiciously, the lady in charge, to wit Mrs. Simeon Slee, allowed the vicar to enter, and then followed him as he went from room to room, making up his mind what he should do as he ran his eye over the proportions of the house, finding in the course of his peregrinations that Mrs. Slee had installed herself in the dining-room, which apparently served for kitchen as well, and had turned the pretty little drawing-room, opening into a shady verandah and perfect wilderness of a garden, into a very sparsely furnished bed-room.

"That will do," said the vicar. "I suppose I can get some furniture in the town?"

"Oh, yes, yow can get plenty furniture if you've got t'money. Only they wean't let yow have annything wi'out. They don't like strangers."

"I dare say I can manage what I want, Mrs. —Mrs.— What is your name?"

"Hey?"

"I say, what is your name?"

"Martha," said the woman, as if resenting an impertinence.

"Your other name. I see you are a married woman."

He pointed to the thin worn ring on her finger.

"Oh, yes, I'm married," said the woman, bitterly; "worse luck."

"You have no children, I suppose?"

. "Not I."

"I am sorry for that."

"Sorry? I'm not. What should I have children for? To pine; while their shack of a father is idling about town and talking wind?"

"They would have been a comfort to you, may be," said the vicar, quietly. "I hope your husband does not drink?"

"Drink?" said the woman, with a harsh laugh. "Yes, I almost wish he did more; it would stop his talking."

"Is he a workman—at the foundry?"

"Sometimes, but Mr. Dicky Glaire's turned him off again, and now he's doing nowt."

"Never mind, don't be downhearted. Times mend when they come to the worst."

"No, they don't," said the woman, sharply.
"If they did they'd have mended for me."

"Well, well," said the vicar; "we will talk
about that another time;" and he took the
two pieces of slag from his pocket, and placed
them on the mantelpiece of the little study,
where they were now standing.

"Some one threw them at yow?" said the
woman.

"Yes," said the vicar, smiling.

"Just like 'em. They don't like strangers
here."

"So it seems," said the vicar. "But you
did not tell me your name, Mrs.——"

"Slee, they call me, Slee," was the sulky
reply.

"Well, Mrs. Slee," said the vicar, "I have
had a good long walk, and I'm very hungry.
If I give you the money will you get me something to eat, while I go down the town and
order in some furniture for this little room and
the bed-room above?"

"Why, the Lord ha' mussy! you're never coming into the place this how!"

"Indeed, Mrs. Slee, but I am. There's half a sovereign; go and do the best you can."

"But the place ought to be clent before you come in."

"Oh, we'll get that done by degrees. You will see about something for me to eat. I shall be back in an hour. But tell me first, if I want to get into the church, who has the keys?"

"Mr. Budd"—Mrs. Slee pronounced it Bood—"has 'em; he's churchwarden, and lives over yonder."

"What, at that little old-fashioned house?"

"Nay, nay, mun, that's th'owd vicarage. Next house."

"Oh," said the vicar, looking curiously at the little, old-fashioned, sunken, thatch-roofed place. "And who lives there?"

"Owd Isaac Budd."

"Another Mr. Budd; and who is he?"

"Th'other one's brother."

"Where shall I find the clerk—what is his name?" said the vicar.

"Oh, Jacky Budd," said Mrs. Slee. "He lives down south end."

"I'm afraid I shall get confused with so many Budds," said the vicar, smiling. "Is that the Mr. Budd who leads the singing?"

"Oh no, that's Mr. Ned Budd, who lives down town. He's nowt to do wi' Jacky."

"Well, I'll leave that now," said the vicar. "But I want some one to fetch a portmanteau from Churley. How am I to get it here?"

"Mrs. Budd will fetch it."

"And who is she?"

"The Laddonthorpe carrier."

"Good; and where shall I find her?"

"Over at Ted Budd's yard — the Black Horse."

"Budd again," said the vicar. "Is everybody here named Budd?"

"Well, no," said the woman, "not ivery

body; but there's a straange sight of 'em all ower the town, and they're most all on 'em cousins or sum'at. But there, I must get to wuck."

The woman seemed galvanized into a fresh life by the duties she saw before her; and almost before the strange visitor had done speaking she was putting on a print hood, and preparing to start.

"It will make a very comfortable place when I have got it in order," said the vicar to himself, as he passed down the front walk. "Now to find some chairs and tables."

This was no very difficult task, especially as the furniture dealer received a couple of crisp bank-notes on account. In fact, one handtruck full of necessaries was despatched before the vicar left the shop and made up his mind to see a little more of the place before returning to his future home.

Perhaps he would have been acting more wisely if he had sent in a load of furniture and announcements of his coming, with orders for the place to be put in readiness; but the Reverend Murray Selwood was eccentric, and knowing that he had an uncouth set of people to deal with, he had made up his mind to associate himself with them in every way, so as to be thoroughly identified with the people, and become one of them as soon as possible.

His way led him round by the great works of the town—Glaire's Bell Foundry—and as he came nearer, a loud buzz of voices increased to a roar, that to him, a stranger, seemed too great for the ordinary transaction of business; and so it proved.

On all sides, as he went on, he saw heads protruded from doors and windows, and an appearance of excitement, though he seemed in his own person to transfer a good deal of the public attention to himself.

A minute or two later, and he found himself nearing a crowd of a couple of hundred workmen, who were being harangued by a tall thin man, in workman's costume, save that he wore a very garish plaid waistcoat, whose principal colour was scarlet.

This man, who was swinging his arms about, and gesticulating energetically, was shouting in a hoarse voice. His words were disconnected, and hard to catch, but "Downtrodden," — "bloated oligarchs," — "British pluck" — "wucking man"— "slavery"—and "mesters," reached the vicar's ears as he drew nearer.

Suddenly there was a movement in the crowd, and the speaker seemed to be hustled from the top of the stone post which he had chosen for his rostrum, and then, amid yells and hootings, it seemed that the crowd had surrounded a couple of men who had been hemmed in while making their way towards the great gates, and they now stood at bay, with their backs to the high brick wall, while the mob formed a semicircle a few feet from them.

It was rather hard work, and wanted no little elbowing, but, without a moment's hesitation, the vicar began to force his way through the crowd; and as he got nearer to the hemmed in men, he could hear some of the words passing to and fro.

"Why, one of them is my friend, Mr. Richard Glaire," said the vicar to himself, as he caught sight of the pale trembling figure, standing side by side with a heavy grizzled elderly workman, who stood there with his hat off, evidently bent on defending the younger man.

"Yow come out o' that, Joe Banks, an' leave him to us," roared a great bull-headed hammer-man, who was evidently one of the ringleaders.

"Keep off, you great coward," was the answer.

"Gie him a blob, Harry; gie him a blob," shouted a voice.

"My good men — my good men," faltered Richard Glaire, trying to make himself heard; but there was a roar of rage and hatred, and

the men pressed forward, fortunately carrying
with them the vicar, and too intent upon their
proposed victims to take any notice of the
strange figure elbowing itself to the front.

"Where are the police, Banks — the
police?"

"Yah! He wants the police," shouted a
shrill voice, which came from the man in the
red waistcoat. "He's trampled down the rights
of man, and now he wants the brutal mummy-
dons of the law."

"Yah!" roared the crowd, and they pressed
on.

"Banks, what shall we do?" whispered
Glaire; "they'll murder us."

"They won't murder me," said the foreman,
stolidly.

"But they will me. What shall we do?"

"Faight," said the foreman, sturdily.

"I can't fight. I'll promise them anything,"
groaned the young man. "Here, my lads," he
cried, "I'll promise you———"

"Yah! You wean't keep your promises," roared those nearest. "Down with them. Get hold of him, Harry."

The big workman made a dash at Richard Glaire, and got him by the collar, dragging him from the wall just as the foreman, who tried to get before him, was good-humouredly baffled by half-a-dozen men, who took his blows for an instant, and then held him helpless against the bricks.

It would have gone hard with the young owner of the works, for an English mob, when excited and urged to action, is brutal enough for the moment, before their manly feelings resume their sway, and shame creeps in to stare them in the face. He would probably have been hustled, his clothes torn from his back, and a rain of blows have fallen upon him till he sank exhausted, when he would have been kicked and trampled upon till he lay insensible, with half his ribs broken, and there he would have been left.

"Police! Where are the police?" shouted the young man.

"Shut themselves up to be safe," roared a lusty voice; and the young man grew dizzy with fear, as he gazed wildly round at the sea of menacing faces screaming and struggling to get at him.

As he cowered back a blow struck him on the forehead, and another on the lip, causing the blood to trickle down, while the great hammer-man held him forward, struggling helplessly in his grasp.

At that moment when, sick with fear and pain, Richard Glaire's legs were failing him, and he was about to sink helpless among his men, something white seemed to whiz by his ear, to be followed instantly by a heavy thud. There was a jerk at his collar, and he would have fallen, but a strong arm was thrown before him; and then it seemed to him that the big workman Harry had staggered back amongst his friends, as a loud voice exclaimed:

"Call yourselves Englishmen? A hundred to one!"

The new vicar's bold onslaught saved Richard Glaire for the moment, and the men fell back, freeing the foreman as they did so. It was only for the moment though, and then with a yell of fury the excited mob closed in upon their victims.

CHAPTER VI.

MOTHER AND SON.

MATTERS looked very bad for the new vicar, and for him he had tried to save, for though the foreman was now ready and free to lend his aid, and Richard Glaire, stung by his position into action, had recovered himself sufficiently to turn with all the feebleness of the trampled worm against his assailants, the fierce wave was ready to dash down upon them and sweep them away.

Harry, the big hammerman, had somewhat recovered himself, and was shaking his head as if to get rid of a buzzing sensation, and murmurs loud and deep were arising, when the shrill voice of the man in the red waistcoat arose.

"Now, lads, now's your time. Trample
down them as is always trampling on you and
your rights. Smite 'em hip and thigh."

"Come on, and show 'em how to do it,"
roared a sturdy voice, and Tom Podmore thrust
himself before the vicar, and faced the mob.
"Come on and show 'em how, Sim Slee; and
let's see as you ain't all wind."

There was a derisive shout at this, and the
man in the red waistcoat began again.

"Down with them, boys. Down with Tom
Podmore, too; he's a sneak—a rat. Yah!"

"I'll rat you, you ranting bagpipe," cried
Tom, loudly. "Stand back, lads; this is
new parson, and him as touches him has to
come by me first. Harry, lad, come o' my
side; you don't bear no malice again a man as
can hit like that."

"Not I," said Harry, thrusting his great
head forward, to stare full in the vicar's face.
"Dal me, but you are a stout un, parson; gie's
your fist. It's a hard un."

It was given on the instant, and the hearty pressure told the vicar that he had won a new ally.

"As for the governor," cried Tom, "you may do what you like wi' him, lads, for I shan't tak' his part."

"Podmore," whispered the vicar, "for Heaven's sake be a man, and help me."

"I am a man, parson, and I'll help you like one; but as for him "—he cried, darting a malignant look at Richard Glaire.

He did not finish his sentence, for at that moment the man in the red waistcoat mounted a post, and cried again:

"Down with 'em, lads; down with——"

He, too, did not finish his sentence, for at that moment, either by accident or malicious design, the orator was upset; and, so easily changed is the temper of a crowd, a loud laugh arose.

But the danger was not yet passed, for those nearest seemed ready to drag their employer from his little body-guard.

"You'll help me then, Podmore?" cried the vicar, hastily. "Come, quick, to the gate."

The veins were swelling in Tom Podmore's forehead, and he glanced as fiercely as any at his master, but the vicar's advice seemed like a new law to him, and joining himself to his defenders, with the great hammerman, they backed slowly to the gate, through the wicket, by which Richard Glaire darted, and the others followed, the vicar coming last and facing the crowd.

The little door in the great gates was clapped to directly, and then there came heavy blows with stones, and a few kicks, followed by a burst of hooting and yelling, after which the noise subsided, and the little party inside began to breathe more freely.

"Thanky, Tom Podmore, my lad," said Banks, shaking him by the hand. "I'm glad you turned up as you did."

Tom nodded in a sulky way, and glowered

at his master, but he pressed the foreman's hand warmly.

" I'd fight for you, Joe Banks, till I dropped, if it was only for her sake ; but not for him."

Meanwhile Harry, the big hammerman, was walking round the vicar and inspecting him, just as a great dog would look at a stranger.

" Say, parson, can you wrastle ? " he said at last.

" Yes, a little," was the reply, with a smile.

" I'd maybe like to try a fall wi' ye."

" I think we've had enough athletics for one day," was the reply. " Look at my hand."

He held out his bleeding knuckles, and the hammerman grinned.

" That's my head," he said. " 'Tis a hard un, ain't it ? "

" The hardest I ever hit," said the vicar, smiling.

" Is it, parson—is it now ? " said Harry, with his massive face lighting up with pride. " Hear that, Tom ? Hear that, Joe Banks ? "

He stood nodding his head and chuckling, as if he had received the greatest satisfaction from this announcement ; and then, paying no heed to the great bruise on his forehead, which was plainly puffing up, he sat down on a pile of old metal, lit his pipe, and looked on.

" I hope you are not hurt, Mr. Glaire ? " said the vicar. " This is a strange second meeting to-day."

" No," exclaimed Richard, grinding his teeth, " I'm not hurt—not much. Banks, go into the counting-house, and get me some brandy. Curse them, they've dragged me to pieces."

" Well, you would be so arbitrary with them, and I told you not," said Banks. " I know'd there'd be a row if you did."

" What ! " cried Richard, " are you going to side with them ? "

" No," said Banks, quietly. " I never sides with the men again the master, and never did ; but you would have your own way about taking off that ten per cent."

" "I'll take off twenty now," shrieked Richard, stamping about like an angry child. "I'll have them punished for this outrage. I'm a magistrate, and I'll punish them. I'll have the dragoons over from Churley. It's disgraceful, it's a regular riot, and not one of those three wretched policemen to be seen."

" I see one on 'em comin'," growled Harry, grinning ; "and he went back again."

" Had you not better try a little persuasion with your workpeople?" said the vicar. " I am quite new here, but it seems to me better than force."

"That's what I tells him, sir," exclaimed Banks, " only he will be so arbitrary."

"Persuasion!" shrieked Richard, who, now that he was safe, was infuriated. "I'll persuade them. I'll starve some of them into submission. What's that? What's that? Is the gate barred?"

He ran towards the building, for at that moment there was a roar outside as if of

menace, but immediately after some one shouted—

"Three cheers for Missus Glaire!"

They were given heartily, and then the gate
bell was rung lustily.

"It's the Missus," said Banks, going towards
the gates.

"Don't open those gates. Stop!" shrieked
Richard.

"But it's the Missus come," said Banks, and
he peeped through a crack.

"Open the gates, open the gates," cried a
dozen voices.

"I don't think you need fear now," said the
vicar; "the disturbance is over for the
present."

"Fear! I'm not afraid," snarled Richard;
"but I won't have those scoundrels in here."

"I'll see as no one else comes in," said
Harry, getting up like a small edition of
Goliath; and he stood on one side of the
wicket gate, while Banks opened it and

admitted Mrs. Glaire, with Eve Pelly, who looked ghastly pale.

Several men tried to follow, but the gate was forced to by the united efforts of Harry and the foreman, when there arose a savage yell; but this was drowned by some one proposing once more "Three cheers for the Missus!" and they were given with the greatest gusto, while the next minute twenty heads appeared above the wall and gates, to which some of the rioters had climbed.

"Oh, Richard, my son, what have you been doing?" cried Mrs. Glaire, taking his hand, while Eve Pelly went up and clung to his arm, gazing tremblingly in his bleeding face and at his disordered apparel.

"There, get away," cried Richard, impatiently, shaking himself free. "What have I been doing? What have those scoundrels been doing, you mean?"

He applied his handkerchief to his bleeding mouth, looking at the white cambric again and again, as he saw that it was stained, and turning very pale and sick, so that he seated himself on a rough mould.

"Dick, dear Dick, are you much hurt?" whispered Eve, going to him again in spite of his repulse, and laying her pretty little hand on his shoulder.

"Hurt? Yes, horribly," he cried, in a pettish way. "You see I am. Don't touch me. Go for the doctor somebody."

He looked round with a ghastly face, and it was evident that he was going to faint.

"Run, pray run for Mr. Purley," cried Mrs. Glaire.

"I'll go," cried Eve, eagerly.

"I don't think there is any necessity," said the vicar, quietly. "Can you get some brandy, my man?" he continued, to Banks. "No, stay, I have my flask."

He poured out some spirit into the cup, and Richard Glaire drank it at a draught, getting up directly after, and shaking his fist at the men on the wall.

"You cowards!" he cried. "I'll be even with you for this."

A yell from the wall, followed by another from the crowd, was the response, when Mr. Selwood turned to Mrs. Glaire.

"If you have any influence with him get him inside somewhere, or we shall have a fresh disturbance."

"Yes, yes," cried the anxious mother, catching her son's arm. "Come into the counting-house, Dick. Go with him, Eve. Take him in, and I'll speak to the men."

"I'm not afraid of the brutal ruffians," cried Richard, shrilly. "I'll not go, I'll——"

Here there was a menacing shout from the wall, and a disposition shown by some of the men to leap down; a movement which had such an effect on Richard Glaire that he allowed his cousin to lead him into a building some twenty yards away, the vicar's eyes following them as they went.

"I'll speak to the men now," said the little lady. "Banks, you may open the gates; they won't hurt me."

"Not they, ma'am," said the sturdy foreman, looking with admiration at the self-contained little body, as, hastily wiping a tear or two from her eyes, she prepared to encounter the workmen.

Before the gates could be opened, however, an ambassador in the person of Eve Pelly arrived from Richard.

"Not open the gates, child?" exclaimed Mrs. Glaire.

"No, aunt, dear, Richard says it would not be safe for you and me, now the men are so excited."

For a few minutes Mrs. Glaire forgot the deference she always rendered to "my son!" and, reading the message in its true light, she exclaimed angrily—

"Eve, child, go and tell my son that there are the strong lock and bolts on the door that his father had placed there after we were besieged by the workmen ten years ago, and he can lock himself in if he is afraid."

The Reverend Murray Selwood, who heard all this, drew in his breath with a low hissing noise, as if he were in pain, on seeing the action taken by the fair bearer of Richard Glaire's message.

"Aunt, dear," she whispered, clinging to Mrs. Glaire, "don't send me back like that —it will hurt poor Dick's feelings."

"Go and say what you like, then, child," cried Mrs. Glaire, pettishly. "Yes, you are right, Eve: don't say it."

"And you will not open the gates, aunt, dear?"

"Are you afraid of the men, Eve?"

"I, aunt? Oh, no," said the young girl, smiling. "They would not hurt me."

"I should just like to see any one among

'em as would," put in Harry, the big hammerman, giving his shirt sleeve a tighter roll, as if
preparing to crush an opponent bent on injur-
ing the little maiden. " We should make him
sore, shouldn't we, Tom Podmore, lad ? "

"Oh, nobody wouldn't hurt Miss Eve, nor
the Missus here," said Tom, gruffly. And then,
in answer to a nod from Banks, the two workmen threw open the great gates, and the yard
was filled with the crowd, headed by Sim Slee,
who, however, hung back a little—a movement
imitated by his followers on seeing that Mrs.
Glaire stepped forward to confront them.

CHAPTER VII.

MRS. GLAIRE'S SPEECH.

" IT's all raight, lads," roared Harry, in a voice of thunder. " Three cheers for Missus Glaire ! "

The cheers were given lustily, in spite of Sim Slee, who, mounting on a pile of old metal, began to wave his hands in' protestation.

" Stop, stop ! " he cried ; " it isn't all raight yet. I want to know whether we are to have our rights as British wuckmen, and our just and righteous demands 'corded to us. What I want to know is——"

" Stop a moment, Simeon Slee," said Mrs. Glaire, quickly ; and a dead silence fell on the crowd, as her clear, sharp voice was heard. ' ' When I was young, I was taught to look a home first. Now, tell me this — before you began to put matters straight for others, did you make things right at home ?"

There was a laugh ran through the crowd at this; but shaken, not daunted, the orator exclaimed—

"Oh, come, that wean't do for me, Mrs. Glaire, ma'am—that's begging of the question. What I want to know is——"

"And what I want to know is," cried Mrs. Glaire, interrupting, "whether, before you came out here leading these men into mischief, you provided your poor wife with a dinner ?"

"Hear, hear," — "That's a good one," — "Come down, Sim,"—"The Missus is too much for ye !" were amongst the shouts that arose on all sides, mingled with roars of laughter; and Sim Slee's defeat was completed by Harry, the big hammerman, who, incited thereto by Banks, shouted—

"Three more cheers for the Missus ! "

These were given, and three more, and three

more after that, the workmen forgetting for
the time being the object they had in view in
the defeat of Simeon Slee, who, vainly trying
to make himself heard from the hill of old
metal, was finally pulled down and lost in the
crowd, while now, in a trembling voice, Mrs
Glaire said—

"My men, I can't tell you how sorry I am
to find you fighting against the people who
supply you with the work by which you live."

"Not again you, Missus," cried half a dozen.

"Yes, against me and my son—the son of
your old master," said Mrs. Glaire, gathering
strength as she proceeded.

"You come back agen, and take the wucks,
Missus," roared Harry. "Things was all raight
then."

"Well said, Harry; well said," cried Tom
Podmore, bringing his hand down on the
hammerman's shoulder with a tremendous slap.
"Well said. Hooray!"

There was a tremendous burst of cheering,

and it was some little time before Mrs. Glaire could again make herself heard.

"I cannot do that," she said, "but I will talk matters over with my son, and you shall have fair play, if you will give us fair play in return."

"That's all very well," cried a shrill voice; and Sim Slee and his red waistcoat were once more seen above the heads of the crowd, for, put out of the gates, he had managed to mount the wall; "but what we want to know, as an independent body of sittizens, is——"

"Will some on yo' get shoot of that chap, an' let Missus speak," cried Tom Podmore.

There was a bit of a rush, and Sim Slee disappeared suddenly, as if he had been pulled down by the legs.

"I don't think I need say any more," said Mrs. Glaire, "only to ask you all to come quietly back to work, and I promise you, in my son's name——"

"No, no, in yours," cried a dozen.

"Well," said Mrs. Glaire, "in my own and your dead master's name—that you shall all have justice."

"That's all raight, Missus," cried Harry. "Three more cheers for the Missus, lads!"

"Stop!" cried Mrs. Glaire, waving her hands for silence. "Before we go, I think we should one and all thank our new friend here —our new clergyman, for putting a stop to a scene that you as well as I would have regretted to the end of our days."

Mrs. Glaire had got to the end of her powers here, for the mother stepped in as she conjured up the trampled, bleeding form of her only son; her face began to work, the tears streamed down her cheeks, and, trembling and sobbing, she laid both her hands in those of Mr. Selwood, and turned away.

"Raight, Missus," roared Harry, who had certainly partaken of more gills of ale than was good for him. "Raight, Missus. Parson hits harder nor any man I ever knowed. Look here, lads, here wur a blob. Three cheers for new parson !"

He pointed laughingly to his bruised forehead with one hand, while he waved the other in the air, with the result that a perfect thunder of cheers arose, during which the self-instituted, irrepressible advocate of workmen's rights made another attempt to be heard ; but his time had passed, the men were in another temper, and he was met with a cry raised by Tom Podmore.

"Put him oonder the poomp."

Simeon Slee turned and fled, the majority of the crowd after him, and the others slowly filtered away till the yard was empty.

CHAPTER VIII.

DEAR RICHARD.

" TAKE my arm, Mrs. Glaire," said the vicar, gently; and, the excitement past, the over-strung nerves slackened, and the woman reasserted itself, for the doting mother now realized all that had gone, and the risks encountered. Trembling and speechless, she suffered herself to be led into the counting-house, and placed in a chair.

" I—I shall be—better directly," she panted.

" Better ! " shrieked her son, who was pacing up and down the room; " better ! Mother, it's disgraceful ; but I won't give way a bit —not an inch. I'll bring the scoundrels to reason. I'll——"

" Dick, dear Dick, don't. See how ill poor aunt is," whispered Eve.

H 2

" I don't care," said the young man, furiously. " I won't have it.   I'll——"

" Will you kindly get a glass of water for your mother, Mr. Glaire ? " said the vicar, as he half held up the trembling woman in her chair, and strove hard to keep the disgust he felt from showing in his face—" I am afraid she will faint."

"Curse the water !   No," roared Richard. "I won't have it—I—I say I won't have it; and who the devil are you, that you should come poking your nose into our business ! You'll soon find that Dumford is not the place for a meddling parson to do as he likes."

" Dick ! " shrieked Eve ; and she tried to lay a hand upon his lips.

"Hold your tongue, Eve !   Am I master here, or not ? " cried Richard Glaire.   " I won't have a parcel of women meddling in my affairs, nor any kind of old woman," he continued, disdainfully glancing at the vicar.

There was a slight accession of colour in

Murray Selwood's face, but he paid no further heed to the young man's words, while, with her face crimson with shame, Eve bent over her aunt, trying to restore her, for she was indeed half fainting; and the cold clammy dew stood upon her forehead.

"Here's a mug o' watter, sir," said the rough, sturdy voice of Joe Banks, as he filled one from a shelf; and then he threw open a couple of windows to let the air blow in more freely.

"Don't let anybody here think I'm a child," continued Richard Glaire, who, the danger passed, was now white with passion; "and don't let anybody here, mother or foreman, or stranger, think I'm a man to be played with."

"There's nobody thinks nothing at all, my lad," said Joe Banks, sharply, "only that if the parson there hadn't come on as he did, you'd have been a pretty figure by this time, one as would ha' made your poor moother shoother again."

" Hold your tongue, sir ; how dare you speak to me like that ! " roared Richard.

" How dare I speak to you like that, my lad?" said the foreman, smiling. " Well, because I've been like a sort of second father to you in the works, and if you'd listened to me, instead of being so arbitrary, there wouldn't ha' been this row."

" You insolent——"

"Oh yes, all raight, Master Richard, all raight," said the foreman, bluffly.

" Dick, dear Dick," whispered Eve, clinging to his arm ; but he shook her off.

" Hold your tongue, will you ! " he shrieked. " Look here, you Bánks," he cried, " if you dare to speak to me like that I'll discharge you ; I will, for an example."

Banks laughed, and followed the raving man to the other end of the great counting-house to whisper :

" No you wean't, lad, not you."

Richard started, and turned of a sickly

hue as he confronted the sturdy old fore-man.

" Think I didn't know you, my lad, eh ? " he whispered ; and driving his elbow at the same time into the young man's chest, he puckered up his face, and gave him a knowing smile. " No, you wean't start me, Richard Glaire, I know. But I say, my lad, don't be so hard on the poor lass there, your cousin."

" Will you hold your tongue ? " gasped Richard. " They'll hear you."

" Well, what if they do ? " said the sturdy old fellow. " Let 'em. There's nowt to be ashamed on. But there, you're popped now, and no wonder. Get you home with your moother."

" But I can't go through the streets."

" Yes, you can ; nobody 'll say a word to you now. Get her home, lad ; get her home."

It was good advice, but Richard Glaire would not take it, and his mother gladly availed her-self of the vicar's arm.

" You'll come home now, Richard," said Mrs. Glaire, feebly; and she looked uneasily from her son to the foreman, as she recalled their conversation in the garden, and felt unwilling to leave them alone together.

"I shall come home when the streets are safe," said Richard, haughtily. "They are safe enough for you, but I'm not going to subject myself to another attack from a set of brute beasts."

"I don't think you have anything to fear now," said the vicar, quietly.

"Who said I was afraid?" snarled Richard, facing sharply round, and paying no heed to the remonstrant looks of cousin and mother. "I should think I know Dumford better than you, and when to go and when to stay."

The young men's eyes met for a moment, and Richard Glaire's shifty gaze sank before the calm, manly look of the man who had so bravely interposed in his behalf.

"Curse him! I hate him," Richard said in

his heart. "He's brave and strong, and big and manly, and he does nothing but degrade me before Eve. I hate him—I hate him."

"What a contemptible cad he is," said Murray Selwood in his heart; "and yet he must have his good points, or that sweet girl would not love him as she evidently does. Poor girl, poor girl! But there: it is not fair to judge him now."

"Of course, you must know best, Mr. Glaire," he said aloud, "for I am quite a stranger. I will see your mother and cousin safely home, and I hope next time we shall have a more pleasant meeting. You are put out now, and no wonder. Good-bye."

He held out his hand with a frank, pleasant smile upon his countenance, and the two women and the foreman looked curiously on as Richard shrank away, and with a childish gesture thrust his hand behind him. But it was of no use, that firm, unblenching eye seemed to master him, the strong, brown muscular hand remained outstretched, and, in spite of himself, the young man felt drawn towards it, and fighting mentally against the influence the while, he ended by impatiently placing his own limp, damp fingers within it, and letting them lie there a moment before snatching them away.

Directly after, leaning on the vicar's arm, and with Eve on her other side, Mrs. Glaire was being led through the knots of people still hanging about the streets. There was no attempt at molestation, and once or twice a faint cheer rose ; but Mr. Selwood was fully aware of the amount of attention they drew from door and window, for the Dumford people were not at all bashful as to staring or remark.

At last the awkward steps were reached, and after supporting Mrs. Glaire to a couch, the new vicar turned to go, followed to the door by Eve.

" Good-bye, and thank you—so much, Mr. Selwood," she said, pressing his hand warmly.

" I did not think we should meet again so soon.
And, Mr. Selwood——"

She stopped short, looking up at him timidly.

"Yes," he said, smiling. "Don't be afraid
to speak ; we are not strangers now."

"No, no ; I know that," she cried, eagerly.
" I was only going to say—to say—don't judge
dear Richard harshly from what you saw this
morning. He was excited and hurt."

" Of course, of course," said the vicar, pressing the little hand he held in both his. " How
could any one judge a man harshly at such a
time ? Good-bye."

" Good-bye."

" And with such a little ministering angel
to intercede for him," muttered the vicar, as
the door closed. " Heigho ! these things are a
mystery, and it is as well that they should be,
or I don't know what would become of poor
erring man."

CHAPTER IX.

AN ENLIGHTENED ENGLISHMAN.

On reaching the vicarage, Murray Selwood found one of the rooms made bright and comfortable with the furniture that had been sent in, and the table spread ready for a composite meal, half breakfast, half dinner, with a dash in it of country tea.

Everything was scrupulously clean, and Mrs. Slee was bustling about, not looking quite so wan and unsociable as when he saw her first.

"I've scratted a few things together," she said, acidly, "and you must mak' shift till I've had more time. Will you have the pot in now? I put the bacon down before the fire when I saw you coming. But, lord, man, what have ye been doin' to your hand?"

"Only bruised it a bit: knocked the skin off," said Mr. Selwood, smiling.

"Don't tell me," said Mrs. Slee, sharply. "You've been faighting."

"Well, I knocked a man down, if you call that fighting," said the vicar, smiling, as he saw Mrs. Slee hurriedly produce a basin, water, and a coarse brown, but very clean, towel, with which she proceeded to bathe his bleeding hand.

"Oh, it's nothing," he said, as he took out his pocket-book. "You'll find scissors and some sticking-plaister in there."

"I don't want no sticking-plaister," she said, taking a phial of some brown liquid from inside a common ornament. "This'll cure it directly."

"And what may this be?" said the vicar, smiling, as he saw his leech shake the bottle, and well soak a small piece of rag in the liquid.

"Rag Jack's oil," said Mrs. Slee, pursing up her lips, and then anointing and tying up the injured hand. "It cures everything."

The vicar nodded, not being without a little faith in homely country simples; and then the rag was neatly sewed on, and an old glove cut so as to cover the unsightly bandage.

"Did they upset you?" she then queried.

"Well, no," he said; and he briefly related what had taken place. "By the way, I hope that gentleman in the red waistcoat is no relation of yours. Is he?"

"Is he?" retorted Mrs Slee, viciously dabbing down a dish of tempting bacon, with some golden eggs, beside the crisp brown loaf and yellow butter. "Is he, indeed! He's my master."

Mrs. Slee hurried out of the room, but came back directly after.

"You've no spoons," she said, sharply; and then making a dive through her thin, shabby dress, she searched for some time for a pocket-hole, and then plunging her arm in right to the shoulder, she brought out a packet tied in a bit of calico. This being undone displayed a paper, and within this another paper was set free. Carefully folded, and fitted into one another, within this were half a dozen very small-sized, old-fashioned silver tea-spoons, blackened with tarnish.

"They are quite clean," grumbled Mrs. Slee, giving a couple of them a rub. "They were my grandmother's, and she gave 'em to me when I was married—worse luck. I keep 'em there so as they shan't be drunk. He did swallow the sugar-tongs."

"Does your husband drink, then?" said Mr. Selwood, quietly.

"Is there anything he don't do as he oughtn't since they turned him out of the plan?" said the woman, angrily. "There, don't you talk to me about him; it makes me wild when I don't want to be."

She hurried out of the room again, shutting the door as loudly as she possibly could without it's being called a bang; and then hunger drove everything else out of the young vicar's mind, even the face of Eve Pelly, and—a minor consideration— his bruised hand.

"A queer set of people indeed," he said, as he progressed with his hearty meal. "What capital bread, though. That butter's delicious. Hah!" he ejaculated, helping himself to another egg and a pinky brown piece of bacon; "if there is any fault in those eggs they are too fresh. By Sampson, I must tell Mrs. Slee to secure some more of this bacon."

Ten minutes later he was playing with the last cup of tea, and indulging it with more than its normal proportions of sugar and milk, for the calm feeling of satisfaction which steals over a hearty man after a meal—a man who looks upon digestion as a dictionary word, nothing more—had set in, and Murray Selwood was thinking about his new position in life.

"Well, I suppose I shall get used to it—in time. There must be a few friends to be made. Hallo!"

The ejaculation was caused by some one noisily entering the adjoining room with—

"Now then, what hev you got to yeat?"

"Nowt," was the reply.

The voices were both familiar, for in the first the vicar recognised that of the man in the red waistcoat — "My master," as Mrs. Slee called him.

"You've been cooking something," he continued loudly.

"Yes.   The parson's come, and it's his brakfast."

"Brakfast at this time o' day! Oh, then, it's him as I see up at foundry wi' them Glaires."

"Don't talk so loud, or he'll hear you," said Mrs. Slee, sharply.

"Let him.   Let him hear me, and let him know that there's a free, enlightened Englishman beneath the same roof. Let him know that there's one here breathing the free—free light—breath of heaven here.   A man too humble to call himself a paytriot, but who feels like one, and moans over the sufferings of his down-trampled brothers."

"I tell you he'll hear you directly, and we shall have to go."

"Let him hear me," shouted Simeon, "and let him drive us out—drive us into the free air of heaven. It'll only be a new specimint of the bloated priesthood trampling down and gloating over the sufferings of the poor. Who's he — a coming down here with his cassicks and gowns to read and riot on his five hundred a year in a house like this, when the hard-working body of brothers on the local plan can preach wi'out having it written down, and wi'out cassicks and gowns, and get nothing for it but glory! Let him hear me."

"Thou fulsome! hold thy stupid tongue," cried Mrs. Slee.

"Never!" exclaimed Simeon, who counted this his opportunity after being baffled in the forenoon. "I'll be trampled on no more by any bloated oligarch of a priest or master. I've been slave too—too long. I'm starving now, but what then? I can be a martyr to a 'holy cause—the 'oly cause of freedom. Let him riot in his food and raiment—let him turn us out, and some day—some day—I say some day——"

Mr. Slee paused in his oratory, for his wife had clapped her hand over his mouth; but just then the door opened, and the vicar stood in the opening.

Mrs. Slee dropped her hand, while Simeon thrust his right into his breast, orator fashion, and faced the new-comer with inborn dignity.

" How do, Mr. Slee," said the vicar, quietly. " We met before this morning. I merely came to say that I cannot help hearing every word that is spoken in this room."

" The words that I said—" began Simeon.

" And," continued the vicar, " I have quite done, if you will clear away, Mrs. Slee. I am going to see about a few more necessaries for the place, and to look out for a gardener, unless your husband likes the job."

"Garden!" said Simeon; "I dig!"

"I often do," said the vicar, coolly. "It's very healthy work. Famous for the appetite. By the way, Mr. Slee, I heard you say you were hungry. Mrs. Slee, pray don't save anything on the table; you are quite welcome."

He walked out of the place, and Mrs. Slee, who, poor woman, looked ravenously hungry, hastened to spread their own table.

"That for you," said Simeon, snapping his fingers after the retreating form. "I care that for you—a bloated priest. Of course, we're to eat his husks—a swine—his leavings. No; I'll rather starve than be treated so."

"Howd thy silly tongue, thou fulsome!" exclaimed Mrs. Slee, "and thank the Lord there is something sent for thee. You talk like that! Oh, Sim, Sim, if ever there was a shack, it's thou."

"Mebbe I am, mebbe I'm not," said Sim, as

he looked curiously on, while his wife filled up the steaming tea-pot, put the half dish of bacon down to warm, and then proceeded to cut some thick slices of bread and butter.

Sim turned his eyes away and tried to look out of the window, but those thick slices, with the holes well filled with butter, were magnetic, and drew his eyes back again.

"I tell ye what, woman," he began, wrenching his eyes away, "that the day is coming when the British wuckman will tear himself from under the despot's heel."

"There, do hold thee clat, and—there, yeat that."

Mrs. Slee thrust a great slice of the tempting bread and butter into her husband's hand, and his fingers clutched it fiercely.

"Yeat that—yeat that?" he cried. "Yeat the bread of a brutal, Church-established tyrant? Yeat the husks of his leavings? Never! I'd sooner—sooner—sooner—sooner—Yah!"

Mr. Simeon Slee's words came more and more

slowly, as he prepared to dash the bread and butter down; but as his eyes rested upon the slice, he hesitated, and as he hesitated he fell, for the temptation was too great for the hungry hero. He uttered a kind of snarling ejaculation, and then treating the bread as if it were an enemy, he bit out of it a great semicircle, while throwing himself into a chair, he sat and ate slice after slice with bacon, in silence, washing all down with cups of tea.

Mr. Slee stirred his tea with a fork-handle, for it was noticeable that the silver teaspoons had disappeared—a line of procedure adopted by Sim as soon as his hunger was appeased, for he had certain meetings of his brotherhood to attend, so he told his wife; and he did not return till late, his coming being announced by sundry stumbles in the passage, and a peculiar thickness of utterance, due doubtless to the exhaustion consequent upon many patriotic utterances at the hostelry known as the Bull for short—the Bull and Cucumber in fact.

Seekers for derivations of signs had puzzled themselves a good deal over the connection between a bull and that familiar gourd of the *cucurbitaceæ* known as a cucumber. It is perhaps needless to add that the learned were baffled, but the incongruity was never noticed by the people of Dumford, and as their pronunciation of the sign was the Bull and Cowcumber, the connection did not sound at all out of place.

Mr. Selwood heard Sim return, and lay for some time listening to his patriotic utterances —fragments, in fact, of the speech he had delivered at the meeting—and it became very evident to the new occupant of the vicarage that life with Mr. Simeon Slee beneath his roof would not be very pleasant.

"I don't like the idea of turning out the poor woman, either," he said to himself, as he lay turning from side to side, courting the rest that would not come.

" I've been a bit excited to-day, I suppose,"

he muttered; and then he tried all the known recipes short of drugs for obtaining rest, from saying a speech backwards to getting out of bed and brushing his hair.

But sleep would not come till close upon morning, for that face before him was the sweet appealing face of Eve Pelly, and in the stillness of the night he seemed to be hearing her words again and again — "Don't judge dear Richard harshly from what you saw this morning."

"Dear Richard, dear Richard, dear Richard" —he found himself repeating over and over again. "And she loves him, and believes in him. He is everything to her, and if she found out that he was a scoundrel it would break her heart."

"And set her free," something in the corner of his own seemed to whisper; and he started, and sat up in bed with the perspiration standing on his brow.

"Am I sane? Am I in my right senses?"

he said, feeling his pulse and counting its beats. " I must be a little out of tone. Humph! I'll have such a walk to-morrow! Bah! it's the excitement of coming down here, and it has been rather a lively day."

He punched and turned his pillow fiercely, threw himself down, and closed his eyes once more, shutting out the dimly-seen lattice window, with its fringe of ivy leaves; but as he did so there was Eve Pelly's face again, and that gentle look which accompanied the appealing curve of her lips, as she said, " Don't judge dear Richard harshly."

The would-be sleeper started up in bed again, and sat there feeling hot and feverish for some time.

" Look here, Murray, dear boy," he said at last. " You are down here for a great purpose. You have here in your charge some four thousand souls to teach and tend, and help on in life's course. Don't fidget, my boy. I'm not going to preach, only to say a few words to the

point.   Now, look here: You are the spiritual
head of the parish; you have your Master's
work to do.   In short, you are a teacher.   Now
mind this, a teacher who cannot govern himself is a broken reed.   Are you a broken reed?"

This was all said in a low voice, and then
for a few moments there was silence in the
room, to be broken by the young man saying
in a somewhat louder voice in answer to his
own words:

"I hope not."

"Good," he continued, in the former tone.
"I like that: it sounds humble and hopeful.
Now look here, you will see a great deal of
what goes on in this place.   In fact, you have
seen a good deal already, and you have learned
what is the state of affairs with one of the
principal families.   You have heard that
Richard Glaire is engaged to his cousin; that
the said cousin loves him; and that this weak
young man is playing fast and loose."

"Yes."

"Good. Well, your duty is plain; the young fellow doubtless has his good points. Make him your friend, and improve them—for her sake—gain an influence over him. You can, and you will, Murray Selwood. Yours may be a hard duty, but you must do it."

"Yes, verily, and by God's help so I will."

"Good. Now you may go to sleep."

After this he lay down, and by a strange exercise of will, and in the belief that he was going to conquer a feeling absolutely new to him, he fell asleep directly.

But it was no peaceful rest such as generally came to his pillow, for he lay tossing in dreams of Eve Pelly turning to him constantly for help from some great trouble that was ever pursuing her—a danger that he could not avert. Then Richard Glaire had him by the throat, charging him with robbing him of his love; and then he was engaged in a mad struggle with the young man, holding him over a gulf to hurl him in, incited thereto by the young workman.

Then once more Eve Pelly's appealing face was before him, praying him to spare dear Richard, the man she loved, and then——

"Thank God, it's morning!" he exclaimed, waking with a start, to consult his watch, and finding it was half-past six.

CHAPTER X.

SIM SLEE BUSY.

BANKS, the foreman, stayed late at the foundry on the night of the disturbance. His master remained in the counting-house smoking cigars till he was very white and ill, feelings which he attributed to the assault made upon him that day—a very sudden one by the way, and one which had arisen, as has been intimated, on account of a rather unfair reduction that had been made in the rate of pay.

But this was not all, for the fact was, that after being left to go on in its quiet, old-fashioned way for years, probably from its insignificance, Dumford had suddenly been leavened by Sim Slee with a peculiar version of his own of the trades-union doctrines of some of the larger towns—doctrines which he had altered to suit his own ends.

Hence arose a society which was the pride of Sim Slee, and known amongst the workmen as the Brotherhood. Meetings were held regularly, speeches made, and Simeon Slee, who heretofore had confined himself to idleness, drink, and local preaching, till expelled as a disgrace to the plan, became a shining light in the brotherhood, on account of what the more quiet workmen called his power of putting things, though the greater part held aloof, from the contempt in which this leader was held.

In previous days, with one or two exceptions, the word of the master of the works had been law, and wages were raised or lowered as trade flourished or fell, with nothing more than a few murmurs; but now times were altered, men had begun to think for themselves, and the behaviour of Richard Glaire had grown so arbitrary and unjust that the consequence was the riot we have seen.

Richard Glaire was about as unsuitable a person as it is possible to imagine to have such a responsibility as the management of a couple of hundred men; but he did not believe this, and he sat, after the departure of his mother, nursing his wrongs, and making plans for the punishment of his workmen.

At one time he was for having the assistance of the military, but as he cooled down he was obliged to acknowledge that his request would be ridiculed.

Then he determined on getting summonses against about twenty of the ringleaders, whom he meant to discharge.

Once he called Banks, and asked him what it would be best to do.

" Put the wage right again," said the foreman.

Whereupon Richard Glaire turned upon him in a burst of childish passion, and declared that he was in league with the scoundrels who had assaulted him.

"There, I shall go till you've had time to cool down," said Banks, grimly. "Your metal's hot, Master Richard, and it wean't be raight again till you've had a night's rest."

Richard made no reply, but sat biting his lips and making plans till dusk, when he cautiously stole out of the building by a side door, of which he alone had the key.

Banks stayed on for another couple of hours, plodding about the building, examining doors, the extinct forges and furnaces, looking at the bands of the huge lathes, and displaying a curious kind of energy, as by means of a small bull's-eye lantern he peered in and out of all sorts of out-of-the-way places.

"There's no knowing what games Master Sim might try on," he remarked to himself; "blowings up and cutting bands, and putting powther in the furnace holes; he's shack enew for ought, and I dessay some on 'em will be stupid enough to side wi' him. What's that ? "

He stopped and listened, for it seemed to him that he had heard a noise below him in the ground floor.

The sound was not repeated, so he went on cautiously through the great black workshop, with its weird assemblage of shafts, cranks, and bands, looking, in the fitful gleams cast by the lantern, like a torture-chamber in the fabled Pandemonium.

A stranger would have tripped and fallen a dozen times over the metal-cumbered floor ; but every inch and every piece of machinery was so familiar to the foreman that he could have gone about the place blindfold, even as he did once or twice in the dark when he closed his bull's-eye lantern, thinking he heard a noise.

All seemed right in this workshop, so he descended to the foundry, going over it and amongst the furnaces, now growing cold.

Then he threaded his way amongst the sunken moulds for castings; looked up at the cranes, paused before the massive crucibles used for melting bell-metal or ingots for the great steel bells, and ended by stopping again to listen.

"I'll sweer I heerd a noise," he muttered, taking a short constable's staff from his pocket, and twisting its stout leather thong round his wrist. "It will be strange and awkward for somebody if I find him playing any of his tricks here."

He went cautiously on tip-toe in the direction from which the noise had seemed to come, going up a short ladder to a raised portion of the foundry, which formed an open floor where lighter work was done.

He advanced very cautiously in the dark, holding his staff ready to deliver a blow, or guard his head, and the next minute there was the sound of some tool being moved on a bench, and then something alighted at his feet, setting up a soft purring and beginning to rub up against his legs.

" Why, Tommy," he said, "you scar'd me, my boy. It was you, was it? After rats, eh, Tommy? Poor old puss, then."

He turned on his lantern, took a good look round, and then, apparently satisfied, he pulled out an old-fashioned silver watch and consulted its face.

" Eight o'clock, eh? Why, they'll think at home that I'm lost."

As he spoke he made his light play round for a few minutes, and then, apparently satisfied, he put it out, placed the lamp on a shelf, and went out and across the yard to the kind of lodge, where a man was waiting to take the duty of the watchman for the night.

" All raight, Mester Banks?"

" All right, Rolf," was the reply. " I've been all round."

Directly after the old foreman was on his way homeward, but he had hardly taken a dozen strides down the lane under the wall, before the head of Simeon Slee was cautiously raised above the edge of one of the great crucibles, or melting-pots, and then for a time he remained motionless.

"You're a clever one, Joe Banks, you are," he said at last, as he raised himself up and sat on the edge of the great pot. "You can find out everything, yow can ; you can trample on the raights of the British wucking-man, and get the independent spirits discharged, eh ? But you're one of the ungodly bitter ones, and you must be smitten wherever you can. Let's see how the wuck 'll go on to-morrow."

The speaker threw his legs over the side, and then paused to dust his trousers and his coat before proceeding further.

"It's hot lying in hiding there," he mut-tered, pulling off his coat and rolling up his sleeves. "I have to toil and moïl like a slave for the cause."

His next proceeding was to open a great

clasp knife and try its edge, which was keen as that of a razor ; and then, armed with this, and quite as much at home in the works as the foreman, he went about with lithe steps as cautious as a cat, and, cutting through the bands that connected the wheels of the lathes with the great shaft that set them in motion, he dragged them down and piled them together till he had collected a goodly heap.

This was not accomplished all at once, and with ease, for, setting aside the watchfulness with which the task had to be done, and the care to ensure silence, the bands were heavy, hard to cut, and they had to be borne some distance. Altogether it took Sim Slee a good hour's arduous labour, and he perspired profusely. In fact, it washis habit to take more pains to achieve a bad end than would have sufficed to get a good living twice over.

" Phew ! it's hot," he muttered in one of his pauses, during which he ran to the nearest door, and listened. " What a slave I am to the cause."

Then he chuckled and laughed over the mischief he had done, and ended by laboriously dragging all the great leather bands and straps to the uncovered hole of a furnace, down which he dropped them, so that they fell far back from the mouth below, which opened on the stoke-hole ; and he knew that the chances were ten to one that if the present heat did not destroy them, a fire would be lit by the careless stokers, and the bands consumed before they were missed, as, if business were resumed on the following day, the firemen would be there long before the ordinary workers.

" Theer," said Sim, when he had finished, " I wonder what Joe Banks would say now if he knew o' this ? "

He resumed his coat, out of the pocket of which he took a piece of strong line, some fifteen feet long, and walked cautiously, listening the while, towards one of the windows which looked down on the lane, one side of which was formed by the works and the wall of the yard, and from which the little door before mentioned gave access to the proprietor's private room in the counting-house.

Sim Slee had entered by this window, being a light, active man, and he was about to descend from it, and make his escape by hitching the strong light steel hook attached to the end of his rope to the sill, just as he had entered by throwing it up till it caught, it being so constructed that a sharp wave sent along the slackened rope would set it free. But before descending Sim stood, rope in hand, listening, watched by the cat at a respectable distance, that sage black animal being evidently impressed with the fact that the intruder in the works was wonderfully rat - like in his actions.

Tommy did not approach him, nor yet purr, but crouched there watching while Sim stood with one ear close to the window, then sharply turned his head and thrust it out into the night air, drew it back again as sharply, and then cautiously thrust it out once more, so that unseen he could see and listen to what went on below.

For there were two figures just below the opening, and as Sim listened, holding his breath, one of them exclaimed :

" I won't, I won't, Mr. Richard, and you've no business to ask me."

" *Mr.* Richard," said the other, reproachfully ; " I thought it was to be Dick—your own Dick."

" Oh, don't—don't—don't talk like that," sobbed the other. " Oh, I wish I really, really knew whether you meant it all."

" Meant it all, Daisy ! how can you be so cruel, when you know how dearly I love you ? But come into the counting-house, and we can sit there and talk."

" I can't—I won't !" said Daisy ; " and you know you oughtn't to ask me, Mr. Richard. What would father say if he were to hear of it ? "

"Father would only be too pleased," whispered the young man, "for he believes in me, if you don't, Daisy. He'd like you to be my own beautiful darling little wife, that I should make a lady."

"But, do you really, really mean it, Mr. Richard?" said Daisy, with a hysterical sob.

"'Really mean it! Mr. Richard!'" said the young fellow, reproachfully. "Oh, Daisy, have you so mean an opinion of me? Do you take me for a contemptible liar?"

"Oh no, no, no," sobbed the girl; "but they say—I always thought—I believed that you were engaged to Miss Eve."

"A poor puny thing," said Richard, in a contemptuous tone; "and besides, she's my cousin."

"But she thinks you love her," said Daisy.

"Poor thing!" laughed Richard.

"And I believe you love her."

"Indeed I don't, nor anybody else but you, you beautiful little rosebud. Oh, Daisy, Daisy, how can you be so cruel!"

" I'm not, I'm not cruel," sobbed poor Daisy ; " but I want to do what's right."

" Of course," whispered Richard. " But come along, let's go in the counting-house— to my room—it's safer there."

" I won't, I won't," cried Daisy, indignantly. " At such a time of night, too ! You oughtn't to ask me."

" I only asked you for your own sake," said Richard, " because people might talk if they saw you with me here."

" Oh yes," sobbed Daisy ; " and they would. I must go."

" Stop a moment," said Richard, catching her wrist. " Perhaps, too, it was a little for my own sake, because the men are so furious against me."

" Oh yes, I heard," cried Daisy, with her voice shaking ; " but they did not hurt you to-day ? "

" Not hurt me !" said Richard. " Why, they nearly killed me."

" No, no," sobbed Daisy.

" But they did; and they would if I hadn't been rescued."

Daisy suppressed a hysterical cry, and Richard passed his arm round her little waist, and drew her to him.

" Then you do love me a little, Daisy ?" he whispered.

" No, no, I don't think I do," sobbed the girl, without, however, trying to get away. " I believe you were going to meet Miss Eve this morning, and were disappointed because I was there."

" Indeed I was not," said Richard. " But I'm sure you were expecting to see that great hulking hound, Tom Podmore."

" That I was not," cried Daisy, impetuously; " and I won't have you speak like that of poor Tom, for I've behaved very badly to him, and he's a good—good, worthy fellow."

" ' Poor Tom !' " said Richard, with a sigh. " Ah, Daisy, Daisy."

"Don't, Mr. Richard, please," sobbed Daisy. who was crying bitterly.

"'Poor Tom—Mr. Richard,'" said the young man, as if speaking to himself.

"Don't, don't, Mr. Richard, please."

"'Mr. Richard.'"

"Well, Dick, then. But there, I must go now."

"Not just now, darling Daisy," whispered Richard, passionately. "Come with me—here we are close by the door."

"No, no, indeed I will not," cried Daisy, firmly.

"Not when I tell you it isn't safe for me to be in the streets at night, for fear some ruffian should knock out my brains?"

"Oh, Dick, dear Dick, don't say so."

"But I'm obliged to," he said, trying to draw her along, but she still resisted.

"I wouldn't have you hurt for the world," she sobbed; "but, Richard — Dick, do you really, really love me as much as you have said?"

" Ten thousand times more, my darling, or I shouldn't have been running horrible risks to-night to keep my appointment with you."

" And you—you want to make me your wife, Richard—to share everything with you ?"

" You know I do, darling," he cried, in a low, hoarse whisper.

" Then, Dick, dear, it wouldn't be proper respect to your future wife to take me there to your works at this time of night," said the girl, simply, as she clung to him.

" Not when the streets are unsafe ?" he cried.

" Let's part now, directly," said Daisy. " I would sooner die than any one should hurt you, Richard ; but you'd never respect your wife if she had no respect for herself. Good night, Richard."

" There, I was right," he cried, petulantly, as he snatched himself away. " You do still care for Tom."

" No, no, Dick, dear Dick. I don't a bit,

sobbed the girl. "Don't, pray don't, speak to me like that."

"Then will you come with me—only because it isn't safe here?" whispered Richard.

"No, no," sobbed the girl, firmly, "I can't do that, and if you loved me as you said, you wouldn't ask me."

"Bah!" ejaculated Richard, angrily. "Go to your dirty, grimy lout of a lover then;" and as the girl clung to him he thrust her rudely away.

Sim Slee, more rat-like than ever, had been rubbing his hands together with delight, as he looked down at the dimly-seen figures, and overheard every word.

"There'll be a faight, and Dicky Glaire will be bunched about strangely," muttered Sim, as Daisy gave a faint scream, for a figure strode out of the darkness.

"She wouldn't have far to go," said the figure, hoarsely.

"Tom!" cried Daisy, shrinking to the wall.

"Yes, it's Tom, sure enew," said the new-comer. "Daisy Banks, it's time thou wast at home, and I'm goin' to see thee theer."

"How dare you interfere, you insolent scoundrel!" cried Richard, striding forward; but he stopped short as Tom drew himself up.

"Look ye here, Richard Glaire — Mester Richard Glaire," said Tom, hoarsely, "I'm goin' to tak' Daisy Banks home to her father wi'out touching of you; but if yow try to stop me, I'll finish the job as I stopped them lads from doing this morning. Now go home while you're raight, for it wean't be safe to come a step nigher."

Richard Glaire drew back, while the young fellow took Daisy by the wrist, and drew her arm through his own, striding off directly, but stopping as Richard cried:

"You cowardly eavesdropper; you heard every word."

"Just about," said Tom, coolly; "I come to tak' care o' Daisy here; and if she'd said 'Yes,'

by the time yow'd got the key of your private
door theer, I should ha' knocked thee down and
had my foot o' thee handsome face, Mester."

He strode off, Daisy having hard work to
keep up with him, sobbing the while, till they
were near her home, when she made an effort
to cease crying, wiped her eyes, and broke the
silence.

"Did—did you hear what I said, Tom?"
she whispered.

"Ivery word, lass, but I only recollect one
thing."

"What was that?"

"That thou did'st not love me a bit."

Daisy gave a sob.

"You mustn't mind, Tom," she said, in a
low voice, "for I'm a bad, wretched girl."

"I should spoil the face of any man who
said so to me," he said, passionately; and then
he relapsed into his quiet, moody manner.

"There's plenty of better girls than me, Tom,
will be glad to love you," she said.

"Yes," he said, softly, "plenty;" and then with a simple pathos he continued bitterly, "and I've got plenty more hearts to give i' place o' the one as you've 'bout broke."

Daisy's breath came with a catch, and they went on in silence for a time—a silence that the girl herself broke.

"Tom," she said, hoarsely, and he gave quite a start. "Tom, are you going to tell mother and father what you've heard and seen?"

"No, lass," he said, sadly, "I'm not o' that sort. I came to try and take care o' thee, not as I've any call to now. Thou must go thy own gate, for wi' such as thou fathers and mothers can do nowt. If Dick Glaire marries thee, I hope thou'lt be happy. If he deceives thee——"

"What, Tom?" whispered the girl, in an awe-stricken tone, for her companion was silent.

"I shall murder him, and be hung out of my misery," said Tom. "There's your door, lass. Go in."

. I. L

He waited till the door closed upon her, and then strode off into the darkness.

Meanwhile Sim Slee leaned cautiously from the window watching Richard, who stood now just beneath him, grinding his teeth with impotent rage as he saw Daisy disappear.

"Why didn't that fool smash the lungeing villain!" said Slee to himself; and then he leaned a little further out.

"I'd like to drop one of these ingots on his head, only it would be mean —Yah! go on, you tyrant and oppressor and robber of the poor, and—oh, my! what a lark!" he said, drawing in his head as Richard Glaire disappeared, when he threw himself on the floor, hugging himself and rolling about in ecstasy, while the cat on a neighbouring lathe set up its back, swelled its tail, and stared at him with dilated eyes.

"Here's a lark!" said Sim again. "Why, we shall get owd Joe Banks over to our side. Oh yes, of course he sides with the mesters, he does. He hates trades unions, he does. He says my brotherhood's humbug, and he's too true to his master to side wi' such as me. Ho, ho, ho! I shall hev' you, Joe Banks, and you'll bring the rest. I shall hev' you; and if you ain't enrolled at the Bull before a month's out, my name ain't Simeon Slee."

"Let me see," said Sim, sitting up sedately and brushing the dirt from his coat, "I've to speak at Churley o' Tuesday. I'll let 'em have it about suthing as 'll fit exact to the case. An' it's a wonderful power is speech. Hey! that it is."

He looked out and listened for a few minutes, and then, all being apparently clear, he placed his knee on the window-sill, slid down the rope, gave it a jerk which set the hook free, caught it nimbly, and rolling the line up, went on preening and brushing himself still like a rat till he reached the Bull and Cucumber, where he was received by the party assembled with a good deal of pot-rattling on the table.

It fell to him, as has been intimated, to

L 2

make a speech or two that night, for the affairs of the day were largely discussed ; and in the course of his delivery he named no names, he said, leastwise he did not say it weer, nor he didn't say it weern't Joe Banks, foreman at the foundry, but what he did say was that there was more unlikely things on the cards than for a certain person to jine their ranks, and become one of a brotherhood of which every man there was proud.

"Well, I don't know so much about that, Sim Slee," said one of the men. "This here don't seem like the societies that we hear on."

"What do you mean ?" said Sim.

"Mean! Why, as instead of our being joined sensible like to get what's reasonable fro' the master, we comes here to hear thee spout."

"That's your ignorance, Peter Thorndike," said Sim. "Yow'd like to be head man pr'haps, and tak' the lead."

"Nay," said the man, "I want to tak' no

leads, for I can't talk like thee; but I want what's sensible and raight for both sides, and I don't see as we're agoing to get it by calling ourselves brothers, and takking oaths, and listening to so much o' thy blather."

"Peter Thorndike," said Sim, folding his arms like an image of Napoleon at St. Helena, "thou'rt only a child yet, and hast much to learn. Don't I tell thee as afore long Joe Banks 'll be over on our side, and a great time coming for Dicky Glaire?"

"Yes, you telled me," growled the man, "but I don't know as I believe it. I wants what's fair, and that's what we all wants, eh, lads?"

"Yes, yes," chorused the others.

"Then you shall have it," said Sim, raising one hand to speak.

"I' words," said Thorndike, "and they don't make owt to yeat. Sim Slee, your brother-hood's all a sham."

CHAPTER XI.

MRS. GLAIRE'S VICTORY.

TEA had been waiting for some time at the house before Richard Glaire made his appearance—for he had of late insisted upon over-setting the old-fashioned homely customs of his boyhood, and dined late.

The drawing-room looked pleasant, for it was well lighted; the tea-service was bright and handsome; and Eve's hand was visible in many places about the room, where flowers were prettily arranged in vases; in the hand-somely-worked cosy which covered the teapot; and in the various pieces of needlework that had grown from her leisure time.

Mrs. Glaire, still somewhat upset by the excitement of the day, was lying on a couch, with her face screened from the lamp, whose soft light fell upon Eve as she sat trying to read, but with her thoughts wandering far away. In fact, from time to time she glanced towards the window, and at every sound a bright look of pleasure took that of the anxiety depicted upon her sweet young face.

Then the animation would die out, and she sat apparently listening.

A sigh from the couch aroused her; and, crossing the room, she bent down to tenderly stroke the grey curls back from Mrs. Glaire's forehead before kissing her.

"Poor aunty," she cooed; "she does want her tea so badly. Let me give you one—just one little cup."

"No, Eve," said Mrs. Glaire; "I'll wait till Richard comes."

"Where can he be?" said Eve, anxiously. "How late he is." Then seeing how her words had impressed her aunt, she hastened to add: "Don't fidget, aunt dear; he's only stopping to have a cigar. He'll soon be here."

"Eve, my child," said Mrs. Glaire, who had been brooding over a trouble other than that which had disturbed her during the day, "bring a stool and sit down by me."

Eve hastened to obey, and, drawing the young girl's head down to her breast, Mrs. Glaire went on :

"My child, you must not think me strange; but I want to talk to you—about Richard."

"Yes, aunt," said Eve, whose voice suddenly turned husky, as her heart began to accelerate its motion.

"You love Dick, Eve ? "

"Oh, aunt dear, yes," faltered the girl, with tears rising to her eyes.

"Of course you do, child. No girl could help loving my son."

"Oh no, aunt."

"I always meant him to marry you here,

my dear; for it would be best for both of you. You have always looked upon him as to be your husband."

"Yes, aunt dear, always."

"Yes, and it will be best for you both," said Mrs. Glaire, repeating herself, as if she found some difficulty in what she had to say.

There was silence then for a few minutes, during which the tea-urn went on humming softly, and both women listened for the truant's footsteps, but he did not come.

"Richard is quite a man now," said Mrs. Glaire, after clearing her throat.

"Yes, aunt dear, quite."

"Does he—does he ever talk much to you about—about love?"

"Oh no, aunt dear," said Eve, in a surprised tone. "But he is always very, very kind to me, and of course he does love me very much. He would never think of talking about it, aunt dear; he shows it."

"Yes, yes, of course," said Mrs. Glaire.

"But—but—does he ever talk to you about —being married ?"

"Married, aunt ?   Oh no ! "

"He ought to," said Mrs. Glaire, with a sigh.   " Eve, my child, I think it would be better for you both if you were married."

"Do you, aunt ; why ?" said Eve, naïvely.

"It would be better for me too," said Mrs. Glaire, evading the question.

"Would it, aunt ? " said Eve, looking at her for a moment, and then hanging her head as if in deep thought.

"Yes, my dear, I should feel happier—I should feel that Richard was settled.   That he had a good, true, dutiful wife, who would watch over him and guide him when I am gone."

"Oh, aunty, aunty, aunty," cried the girl, turning and twining her arms round her neck to kiss her tenderly, "you are low-spirited and upset with that terrible trouble to-day. You must not talk like that.   Why, you look so

young and bright and happy sometimes, that
it's nonsense for you to say dear Dick wants
some one to look after him. Of course we
shall be married some day—when Dick likes;
but we never think of such a thing—at least,
I'm sure I don't."

There was a pleasant, rosy flush on the girl's
face as she spoke, and just then a cough in the
hall made her jump up, exclaiming—

"Here's Dick!"

Mr. Richard Glaire swung the door open
directly after, gave a scowl round the room,
nodded shortly at his mother, threw himself
into an easy-chair, picked up the book Eve had
been reading, glanced at it, and with an impatient "pish!" jerked it to the other side of
the room.

Eve laughed, made a pretty little grimace
at him, and, removing the cosy, hastened to
pour out the tea, one cup of which she held
ready, evidently expecting that Richard would
come and take it to his mother. Then, seeing

that he did not pay any heed to her look, she carried the cup herself, round by the back of the young man's chair, giving his hair a playful twitch as she went by.

"Don't!" shouted Richard, angrily, and then in an undertone muttered something about "confounded childishness," while Eve bent over her aunt and whispered softly—

"He'll be better when he has had some tea, aunt dear. He's upset with thinking about to-day."

Mrs. Glaire nodded, and watched the pretty, graceful form as Eve tripped back, to stand for a moment or two behind Richard's chair, resting her hands upon his shoulders as she whispered tenderly—

"Does your face hurt you, Dick dear?"

"Bother!" growled Dick, pouring the cup of tea to which he had helped himself down his throat. "Here, fill this."

Eve took the cup and saucer, only smiling back at him, and refilling it, said playfully—

"Dick's cross, aunty. I'm going to give him double allowance of sugar to sweeten his temper."

"I wish you'd pour out the tea, and not chatter so," he cried, impatiently. "What with your tongue and hers, there isn't a bit of peace to be had in the place."

Eve looked pained, but the look passed off, and without attending to her own wants, she took some bread and butter across to where Richard sat scowling at the wall.

"Won't you have something to eat, Dick dear?" she said, affectionately.

"NO!"

There are a good many ways of saying "no." This was one of the most decisive, and was uttered so sharply that Eve forbore to press that which she had brought upon her cousin, and carried it to her aunt.

The rest of the time before retiring was passed in about as agreeable a way, till, at a nod from Mrs. Glaire, Eve said, "Good night," being affectionately embraced by her aunt, and then turning to Dick, she bent over him.

" Good night, dear Dick," she whispered, holding her cheek to be kissed, as she rested her hands upon his shoulders.

" There, good night. For goodness' sake don't paw one about so."

Eve remained motionless, with the tears gathering in her eyes, for a few moments, before bending down and kissing the young man's forehead.

" Good night, dear darling Dick," she whispered. " I'm very sorry about all your troubles; but don't speak like that, it — it hurts me."

The next moment she had taken up her candlestick and glided from the room.

Richard Glaire gave himself an impatient twist in his chair, and lay back thinking of the warm, glowing beauties of Daisy Banks, when he started up in affright, so silently had his mother risen from her couch, advanced, laid her hands upon his shoulder, one crossed over the other, and said in a low, clear voice—

"Dick, you are thinking of Daisy Banks."

"I—I thought you were asleep," he stammered.

"I was never more wide awake, Richard—to your interests," said Mrs. Glaire.

"I don't know what you mean," he said, petulantly, as he gave the lamp-shade a twist, so that its light should not fall upon his face, and then changed his position a little.

"Yes, you do, Richard—perfectly," said Mrs. Glaire. "I said just now that you were thinking of Daisy Banks."

"Yes, I heard you say so; and I said, I don't know what you mean."

An angry retort was upon Mrs. Glaire's lips, but she checked the hasty expression, and pressing her hands a little more firmly upon her son's shoulders, she went on—

"You know perfectly well what I mean,

Richard, and I must speak to you about that, as well as about the business."

"Look here," exclaimed the young man, impatiently ; "I'm tired and worried enough for one day. I'm going to bed."

He started up, crossed to the side table, took a candle, and advancing to the lamp, was about to light it with a taper, when, to his surprise, his mother, who of late years had given up to him in everything, took candle and taper from his hands and pressed him back unresisting into his seat.

"Richard, you are not going to bed till you have heard what I have to say."

"I tell you I'm worn out and worried !" he exclaimed.

"You were not too tired to go out and keep engagements," said Mrs. Glaire, firmly.

"Who told you I had been out to keep engagements ? " retorted Richard, sharply.

"My heart, Richard," said his mother. "I know as well as if I had seen you that

you have been to-night to meet Daisy
Banks."

"What stuff, mother!"

"As you have often been to meet her,
Richard; tell me, do you wish to marry
her?"

"I marry that hoyden — that workman's
daughter! Mother, are you mad?"

"You are only a workman's son, sir."

"My father made me a gentleman, mother,"
said Richard, taking out a cigarette, "and I
have the tastes of a gentleman. May I light
this?"

"Smoke if you wish to, Richard," said Mrs.
Glaire, quietly. "I have never stood in your
way when that was a just one."

Richard lit his cigarette, threw himself back
in his chair with one leg over an arm, and said
negligently—

"Well, if I am to be lectured, go on."

"I am not going to lecture you, my son,"
said Mrs. Glaire, firmly; "I am only interpos-

ing when I see you hesitating on the brink of a precipice."

"Look here, mother," cried Richard; "do you want to quarrel?"

"No, Richard, to advise."

"Then don't talk stuff, mother."

"I shall not, Richard, neither shall I let you put me off in what I wish to say. I am going to speak to you about Joseph Banks' daughter, and about the business."

"Now, look here, mother," cried the young man, who, with all his desire to go, felt himself pinned down in his chair by a stronger will—"look here. What stuff have you got in your head about that little girl?"

"The stuff, as you call it, that is the common talk of the town."

"Oh, come, that's rich," cried Richard, with a forced laugh. "To keep me up here and scold me about the common talk of scandal-mad Dumford. Mother, I thought you had more sense."

"And I, Richard, thought that you had more honour; that your father had brought you up as a gentleman; and that you really had the tastes of a gentleman."

"Come, I say, this is coming it too strong, you know, mother," said the young man, in a feeble kind of protestation. "It is too hard on a fellow: it is indeed, you know."

"Richard," continued Mrs. Glaire, with her words growing more firm and deep as she proceeded, "I have had Daisy Banks in this house off and on for years, as the humble companion of Eve, who is shut out here from the society of girls of her own age. It was a foolish thing to do, perhaps, but I was confident in the honour and gentlemanly feeling of my son, the wealthiest and greatest man in Dumford—in the honour of my son who is engaged to be married to his second cousin, Eve Pelly, as good, pure-minded, and sweet a girl as ever lived."

"Oh, Eve's right enough," said Richard,

M 2

roughly, "or she ought to be, for I'm sick of hearing her praises."

" A girl who loves you with her whole heart, and who only waits your wishes to endow you with the love and companionship that would make you a happy man to the end of your days."

" Oh yes," said Richard, yawning. " I know all about that."

" And what do I wake up to find ?"

"Goodness knows, mother; some mare's nest or another."

" I wake up to find what Joseph Banks, our trusty old foreman, also wakes up to find."

" What !," roared Richard, thrown off his balance; " does he know ? "

" Yes," said Mrs. Glaire; " he, too, knows. Does that touch you home ? "

" D——n !" muttered Richard, between his teeth.

" Yes, Banks too has woke up to the fact that you are frequently seen alone, and in a clandestine manner, with his only child; but he believes that you love her, that you, in spite of your position, remember that you are only a workman's son, and that you mean to marry a workman's daughter, and bring her home here as the wife of the master of Dumford Works."

"Confound it all!" muttered Richard, biting his nails.

"He smiles at the notion of your being engaged to Eve, for he believes you to be honourable and a gentleman, while I, your mother, am obliged to know that your designs are evil, that you plot the ruin of a poor, weak girl—I wake up, in short, to know that my son is behaving like a scoundrel."

"Hold your tongue!" cried Richard, hoarsely; and leaping up, he took two or three turns backwards and forwards in the room, before throwing himself once more in his chair.

"But you've not spoken to Joe Banks?" he cried.

"I have, this morning," said Mrs. Glaire, and then, her voice trembling, and the judge-like tone giving way to one of appeal, she threw herself at the young man's knees, clasping them with her arms, and then catching at and holding his hand. "Dick, my boy—my darling—I was obliged to speak—I *am* obliged to speak to you. You know how, since you became of age, I have delivered everything into your hands—how I have kept back from interfering—how I have been proud to see the boy I brought into the world rich and powerful. You know I have never stood in the way, though you have poured out like water on your betting and gambling the money your father and I saved by dint of scraping and saving."

"Oh, that's it, is it?" said Richard, with a sneer.

"No," cried his mother, appealingly, "it is not, Dick, my boy; it is that I wish to make you see your danger before it is too late. You

mad, infatuated boy, can you not see that by
what you have done you have set all your
workmen against you?   You see how you are
treated to-day!"

"Oh yes," said Richard; "and I've got the
marks upon me."

"Who stood by you, faithfully and true, as
he has always stood by our house in similar
times of danger—danger not brought on by
folly?—Banks, your father's old fellow-work-
man—a man as true as steel."

"Oh yes, Joe Banks is right enough," muttered Richard.

"And yet you, Dick—oh, Dick, Dick, my
boy, think what you are doing — you would
reward him for his long services by doing him
the greatest injury man could do to man.   Are
you mad?"

"If I'm not, you'll drive me mad," cried
Richard, trying to shake off his mother's tight
embrace.

"No, no, Dick, you shall not leave me yet,"

cried Mrs. Glaire, in impassioned tones, as the tears now streamed down her cheeks. "You must—you shall listen to me. Can you not see that besides maddening the poor man by the cruel wrong you would do, you will make him your deadly enemy; that the works would be almost helpless without him; and that he is the strong link that holds the workpeople to our side? For they respect him, and——"

"Go on. They don't respect me, you were going to say," said Richard, petulantly. "Oh, mother, it's too bad. You've got hold of some cock-and-bull bit of scandal, set about by one of the chattering fools of the place—old Bullivant, very likely—and you believe it."

"Richard, my boy," said Mrs. Glaire, rising and standing before him, "can you not be frank and candid with your own mother?"

"You won't let me," he said; "you do nothing but bully me."

"When I tell you of your danger; when I

remind you that you are standing on the edge
of a precipice———"

" Oh, hang the precipice !" he cried ; " you
said that before."

" When I warn you of the ruin, and beg of
you on my knees, my boy, if you like, not to
pursue this girl—not to yield to a weak, mad
passion that will only bring you misery and
regret to the end of your days, for you would
never marry her."

" Well, it isn't likely," he said, brutally.

" Dick—Dick," cried Mrs. Glaire, passionately, roused by the callous tone in which he
spoke, "are you in your right senses, or have
you been drinking ?   It cannot be my boy who
speaks ! "

" Well, there, all right, mother, I'll own to it
all," he said, flippantly, and then he winced as
the poor woman cast her arms round his neck,
and strained him to her breast.

" I knew you would, my boy, as soon as the
good in your nature got the upper hand. And .

now, Dick, you'll promise me you won't see Daisy Banks any more."

"All right, mother, I won't."

"Thank you, Dick. God bless you for this. But I must talk to you a little more. I have something else to say."

"What, to-night?" he said, with a weary yawn.

"Yes, to-night. Just a few words."

"Go on then, only cut it short."

"I wanted to say a few words to you about Eve."

"Oh, bother Eve," he muttered. "Well, go on."

"Don't you think, Dick, my boy, you've been very neglectful of poor Eve lately?"

"Been as attentive as I ever have."

"No, no, Dick; and listen, dear; try and be a little more loving to her."

"Look here, mother," cried Richard, impatiently; "I've promised all you want."

"Yes, yes, my boy."

"Well, if you get always trying to thrust Eve down my throat, I shall go away."

"Richard!"

"I'm tired of being bored about her."

"But your future wife! Dick, my boy—there, only a few more words—will you take my advice?"

"Yes—no—yes; well, there, I'll try."

"Don't you think, then, *that* had better come off soon?"

"*That!* What?"

"Your marriage."

"No, indeed I don't, so I tell you. I don't mean to be tied up to any woman's apron-string till I have had my fling. There, good night; I'm going to bed."

Mrs. Glaire made an effort to stay him, but he brushed by her, turned at the door, said, "Good night," and was gone.

As the door closed, Mrs. Glaire sank into the chair her son had so lately occupied, and sat thinking over their conversation.

Would he keep his word? Would he keep his word? That was the question that repeated itself again and again, and the poor woman brought forward all her faith to force herself to believe in her son's sense of honour and truth, smiling at last with a kind of pride at the victory she had won.

But as she smiled, lighting her candle the while, and then extinguishing the lamp, a shiver of dread passed through her at the recollection of the events of the day; and at last, when she passed from the room a heavy shadow seemed to follow her. It was the shadow of herself cast by the light she carried, but it seemed to her like the shadow of some coming evil, and as she went upstairs and passed her son's door, from beneath which came the odour of tobacco, she sighed bitterly, and went on wondering how it would end, for she had not much faith in his promise.

CHAPTER XII.

MORE TROUBLE AT THE WORKS.

" I SHALL have to do something about these people," said the vicar, as he descended, after making a hasty toilet.

His way out lay through the room appropriated by the objects of his thoughts, and on opening the door it was to find Mr. Simeon Slee's toilet still in progress. In fact, that gentleman was seated in a chair, holding a tin bowl of water, and his wife was washing his face for him, as if he were a child.

They took no notice of the interruption, and the vicar passed through, intending to take a long walk, but he checked his steps at the gate, where he stood looking down the long street, that seemed a little brighter in the early morning.

He had not been there five minutes before he saw a sodden-looking man come out of the large inn—the Bull and Cucumber—and as the pale, sodden-looking man involuntarily wiped his mouth with the back of his hand, the vicar nodded.

"Morning drain, eh? I'm afraid yours is not a very comfortable home, my friend."

The man was going slowly down the street when his eye caught the figure of the vicar, and he immediately turned and came towards him, and touched his hat.

"Mr. Selwood, sir?"

"That is my name, my man."

"I'm Budd, sir—J. Budd — the clerk, sir. Thowt I'd come and ask if you'd like the garden done, sir. I'm *the* gardener here, sir. Four days a week at Mr. Glaire's. Your garden, sir——"

"Would have looked better, Budd, if, out of respect to the church and the new vicar, you had kept it in order."

"Yes, sir; exackly, sir; but I was too busy, sir.   Shall I come, sir?"

"Yes, you may come, Budd.   By the way, do you always have a glass before breakfast?"

"Beg pardon, sir—a glass?"

"Yes, at the Bull?"

"Never, sir," said Budd, with an injured air. "I went in to take Mr. Robinson's peck."

"Peck of what? pease?"

"Peck, sir—peck-axe—maddick."

"Oh, I see," said the vicar, looking at the man so that he winced.   "Well, Budd, come and see to the garden after breakfast."

"That I will, sir."

"And, by the way, Budd."

"Yes, sir."

"Don't wipe your mouth when you have been to return picks or mattocks.   I'm rather a hard, matter-of-fact person, and it makes me think a man has been drinking."

Jacky Budd touched his hat without a word, stuck one thumb into his armhole, and went off to inform the next person he met that "new parson" was a tartar and a teetotaler.

By this time Simeon Slee had gone off in another direction, and as the vicar was busy with his pocket-knife, pruning some trailing branches from the front windows, Mrs. Slee came to announce that his breakfast was ready, and soon after relieved him of a difficulty.

"Going, eh, Mrs. Slee? When?"

"I thowt we'd flit to-day, sir. We only came in to take charge of the house."

"Have you a place to go to?"

"Yes, sir."

"Humph! Well, it's best, perhaps, Mrs. Slee, for I am a frank man, and I don't think your husband and I would agree. You couldn't come and keep me right till I've got a house-keeper, I suppose?"

Mrs. Slee could, and said she would; and that morning Jacky Budd helped the poor woman to "flit" her things to a neighbouring cottage, Simeon vowing that he'd "never set foot in the brutal priest's house again."

"You're well shut of a bad lot, sir," said Jacky Budd, turning to Mr. Selwood, after the last items of the Slee impedimenta were off the premises, and he had looked round the wilderness of a garden, sighed, and wondered how he should ever get it in order.

"Think so, Budd?" said the vicar, drily.

"Yes, sir, I do," said Jacky, resting on the spade he had not yet begun to use; "he's a Ranter, is Slee, a Primity Methody, sir—a fellow as sets up against our Church—helps keep the opposition shop, and supplies small-beer instead of our sacrymental wine."

Jacky involuntarily smacked his lips as he spoke, and the vicar turned sharply upon him with knit and angry brows.

But Jacky Budd was obtuse, and saw it not, but went on, wiping his forehead the while, as if he were panting and hot with his exertions.

"They had him down on the plan, sir; they

did, 'pon my word of honour, sir—him, a regular shack, as never does a day's work if he can
help it. He was a local preacher, and put on a
white 'ankercher o' Sundays, and went over to
Churley, and Raiby, and Beddlethorpe, and
Mardby, and the rest of 'em, he did. It's as
good as a play, sir, to hear him preach. But
they've 'bout fun' him out now."

"You have been to hear him, then, Budd?"
said the vicar, drily.

"Me? Been to hear he? Me, sir—the
clerk of the parish? No, sir; I never be-
meaned myself by going into one of their
chapels, I can assure you," said Jacky, indignantly; and raising his spade, he chopped
down a couple of unorthodox weeds growing
up within the sacred borders of the vicarage
garden.

"I'm glad to hear it, Budd," said Mr. Selwood, looking at him curiously; "and now I
think as you've begun, we'll go on with the
gardening."

"To be sure, sir—to be sure," said Jacky, looking round and sighing at the broad expanse of work; "but if I might be so bold, sir, I should say, Don't you have nowt to do wi' that chap Slee. He's a regular Shimei, sir—a man as curses and heaves stones at our holy Church, sir—a man as comes in the night, and sows tares and weeds amongst our wheat."

"Exactly, Budd," said the vicar, looking him full in the face; "but now suppose we sink the metaphorical and take to the literal. There are tares and weeds enough here: so suppose you root them out of the garden."

"Yes, sir, of course, sir; I was just going to," said Jacky. "It's a lovely garden when it's in good order. I suppose you wouldn't like me to get Thad Warmouth and one of the Searbys to come and help me—labouring chaps, sir, and very strong?"

"No, Budd, I really should not," said the vicar; "and besides, it would be depriving you of a good deal of work. What three men would do in two days will last one man six."

"Exactly, sir—thanky, sir; it's very thowtful of you," said Jacky, sighing, and looking as if he would be willing to be deprived of a good deal of work; and then he began to chop at the ground very softly, as if, knowing that it was his mother earth, he was unwilling to hurt it.

"I'm fond of gardening myself, Budd; it's good, healthy work, and I dare say I shall help you a great deal. Excuse me; lend me that spade a moment. I think it would be as well to drive it right in like this—it will save further trouble; this wild convolvolus takes such a strong hold of the soil."

He took the tool and dug for a few minutes lustily, stooping down after each newly-turned spadeful to pick up and remove the long, white trailing roots that matted it together, horrifying Jacky, who took off his hat and wiped his dewy forehead, for it made him perspire freely to see such reckless use of muscular power.

"Thanky, sir; yes, I see," said Jacky, taking the spade again with a sigh, and fervently wishing that he had not undertaken the job. "Hallo! here's the Missus."

He paused, and rested his foot on the spade, as just then Mrs. Glaire, driving a little four-wheel chaise, drawn by an extremely chubby pony, like a heavy cart-horse cut down, drew up by the vicarage gate.

The little lady was greatly agitated, though she strove hard to keep an equable look upon her countenance, returning the vicar's salute quietly, as he walked down to the gate; whilst such an opportunity of a respite from the spade not being one to be neglected, Jacky Budd stuck that implement firmly amongst the weeds, and followed closely.

"Shall I hold Prinkle, mum?" he said, going to the pony's head.

"Yes—no, Jacky, I'm not going to stay,"

said Mrs. Glaire. "Are you at work here,
then?"

"Yes, mum."

"Mind he does work, then, Mr. Selwood,"
she continued; "and don't let him have any
beer, for he's a terribly lazy fellow."

Jacky looked appealingly at his mistress,
then smiled, and looked at the vicar, as much
as to say, "You hear her—she will have her
joke."

"Is anything the matter?" said the vicar,
earnestly.

"Well, yes; not much, Mr. Selwood: but I
am getting old and nervous, and I thought I
would ask you to come up. You seemed to
have so much influence with the men."

"Certainly I'll come up, if I can be of any
use."

"Pray get in then," said Mrs. Glaire, and
the springs of the little vehicle went down as
the vicar stepped in, while, during the minute
or two that ensued, as Mrs. Glaire drove up to

the foundry, she told him that the works had not been opened till mid-day, when it had been agreed upon by her son—at her wish—that he would receive some of the workmen at the counting-house, and try to make some arrangement about terms.

" I went to the works, too," she said, " not to interfere, but to try and be ready to heal any breach that might arise. Of course I called in as if by accident, as I was going for a drive."

"And has anything occurred ? " said the vicar.

" No ; but I was afraid, for Richard is very impetuous, and I thought as—as you saw what you did yesterday——"

" My dear Mrs. Glaire, pray always look upon me as an old friend, who has your welfare and that of the people thoroughly at heart. Oh, here we are."

His remarks were cut short by the pony turning sharply in at the great gates, as if quite accustomed to the place, and as the men, who were pretty thick in the yard, made way, some of them roughly saluting the occupants of the chaise, the pony stopped of its own accord in front of the counting-house.

The vicar sprang out and helped Mrs. Glaire to alight, following her into the building, where Richard was sitting, looking very sulky, at the head of a table, and about a dozen of the men were present, Simeon Slee being in the front rank.

" It's going agen my advice, Mester Richard Glaire," he was saying. " If the men did as I advise, they'd stand out, but I'm not the man to stand in the way of a peaceable settlement, and as you've come to your senses, why I agree."

"I didn't agree for you to come to the works, Slee," said Richard, sharply.

"Yes, yes, yes," chorused half-a-dozen voices; " all or none, Maister. All or none."

"I can stand out," said Sim, loftily. "I can afford to be made a martyr and a scapegoat, and bear the burthen. I don't want to come back to work."

" And I don't want and don't mean to have you," said Richard, hotly. " I sent to you all this morning, forgiving the brutal treatment I met with yesterday——"

" Your own fault," said a voice.

" Howd thee tongue, theer," said one of the men, who seemed to take a leading part. " Bygones is bygones. You sent for us, Maister Richard, and we've come. You says, says you, for the sake o' peace and quiet you'd put wage where it were, and you've done it, but it must be all or none. Fair play's fair play, ain't it, parson ?"

" Yes, yes, Richard, give way," whispered Mrs. Glaire ; and with an impatient stamp of his foot Richard Glaire gave his lip a gnaw, and exclaimed—

" There, very well ; Slee can come back ; but mind this, if he begins any of his games and speech-making in the works again, he goes at once."

"Oh, I can stay away," said Slee, in an injured tone; but his fellow-workmen held to his side, and, to Mrs. Glaire's great relief, an amicable settlement was arrived at, and the men were about to go, when Banks, the old foreman, burst into the place in a towering passion.

"Howd hard theer," he roared, looking fiercely round. "You're a pretty set o' cowardly shacks, you are. Do you call that a fighting fair?"

"What is it, Banks?" exclaimed Richard, starting.

"Don't make no terms wi' 'em at all, for they wean't keep to 'em, the blackguards."

"But what is it?" cried Richard, impatiently.

"What is it? What is it, Missus Glaire? Why, I was watching here mysen till nine o'clock, and left all safe."

"Well?" cried Richard, turning pale.

"Look here, Joe Banks," cried the man who

had been speaking before; "tak' it a bit easy, theer. None o' us ain't done nowt, ha'e we, lads?"

"No," was chorused, Sim Slee's voice being the loudest.

"Done nowt!" roared Banks, like an angry lion. "D'yer call it nowt to steal into a man's place, and coot and carry off every band in t' whole works?"

"Have they—have they done that, Banks?" cried Richard.

"Have they?" roared the foreman; "ask the sneaking cowards."

"No, no, we hain't," cried the leader, bringing his hand down on the table with a thump. "It's a loi, ain't it, lads—a loi?"

"Yes," was chorused; "we ain't done nowt o' t' sort."

"Then who did it?" cried Banks; and there was a silence.

"Look here," cried Richard, who had been brought very unwillingly to this concession by

Mrs. Glaire, and gladly hailed an excuse for evading it. "Look here, Banks, are all those wheel-bands destroyed?"

"Ivery one of 'em," said Banks.

"Then I'll make no agreement," cried Richard, in a rage. "You may strike, and I'll strike. It's my turn now—be quiet, mother, I'm master here," he cried, as Mrs. Glaire tried to check him. "I won't have my property destroyed, and then find work for a pack of lazy, treacherous scoundrels. There's a hundred pounds' worth of my property taken away. Make it up, and put it back, and then perhaps I'll talk to you."

"But I tell you, Mester, it's none o' us," cried the leader.

"None of you!" sneered Richard. "Why, the bands are gone, and I'm to give way, and pay better, and feed you and yours, and be trampled upon. Be off, all of you; go and strike, and starve, till you come humbly on your knees and beg for work."

"Had you not better try and find out the offender, Mr. Glaire?" interposed the vicar, who saw the men's lowering looks. "Don't punish the innocent with the guilty."

"Well spoke, parson," cried a voice.

"You mind your own business, sir," shouted Richard. "I know how to deal with my own workmen. You struck for wages, and you assaulted me. I'll strike now, you cowards, for I'll lock you out. The furnaces are cold; let them stop cold, for I'll lose thousands before I'll give in. I'll make an example of you all."

"You'll repent this, Mester Richard Glaire," shouted Slee.

"I'll repent when I see you in gaol, you mouthing demagogue!" cried Richard. "Now, get off my premises, all of you, for I'll hold no more intercourse with any of the lot."

"But I tell you, Mester," said the leader, a short, honest-looking fellow, "it's——"

"Be off, I tell you!" shouted Richard. "Where are my bands?"

The man wiped his forehead, and looked at his companions, who one and all looked from one to another, and then, as if feeling that there was a guilty man amongst them—one who had, as it were, cut the ground from beneath their feet — they slowly backed out, increasing their pace though, towards the last, as if each one was afraid of being left.

"Go after them, Banks, and see them off the premises," said Richard, with a triumphant look in his eye. "Let's see who'll be master now."

The foreman went after the deputation, and there was a low murmuring in the yard, but the men all went off quietly, and the great gates were heard to clang to.

"Oh, Richard, my boy," said Mrs. Glaire, "I'm afraid you've made matters worse."

"I'll see about that," said Richard, rubbing his hands, and giving a look askant at the vicar, who stood perfectly silent. "They'll be down on their knees before the week's out, as soon as the cupboard begins to be nipped. Are they all gone, Banks ? "

" Yes, they're all gone," said the foreman, returning. " I wouldn't ha' thowt it on 'em."

" Stop ! " cried Richard, as a sudden idea seemed to strike him. " What time did you go away, Joe ? "

" 'Bout nine."

" And all was right then ? "

" That I'll sweer," said the foreman ; " I went all over the works. It must ha' been done by some cowardly sneak as had hid in the place."

" I know who it was," said Richard, with his eyes sparkling with malicious glee.

" Know who it was ? " said Banks. " Tell me, Maister Richard, and I'll 'bout break his neck."

" It was that scoundrel Tom Podmore."

" Who ? Tom Podmore ! Yah ! " said the foreman, in a tone of disgust ; and then with a chuckle. " I dessay he'd like to gi'e you

one, Maister Dick ; but go and steal the bands !
It ain't in him."

"But I tell you I saw him !" cried Richard.

" Saw him ? When ?"

" Hanging about the works here last night
between nine and ten."

" You did ! " cried the foreman, eagerly.

" That I did, myself," said Richard, while
the vicar scanned his eager face so curiously
that the young man winced.

Joe Banks stood thinking with knitted brow
for a few moments, and then, just as Mrs.
Glaire was going to interpose, he held up his
hand.

" Wait a moment, Missus," he said. " Look
here, Maister Richard, you said you saw Tom
Podmore hanging about the works last night ?"

" I did."

" There's nobbut one place wheer a chap
could ha' been likely to ha' gotten in," said
Banks, thoughtfully. " Wheer might you ha'
sin him ?"

" In the lane by the side."

" That's the place," said the foreman, in a disappointed tone. " That theer window. Was he by hissen ? "

" Yes, he was quite alone," said Richard, flinching under this cross-examination.

" And what was you a-doing theer, Maister Richard, at that time ? " said the foreman, curiously.

" I — I —" faltered Richard, thoroughly taken aback by the sudden question ; " I was walking down to go into the counting-house, with a sort of idea that I should like to see if the works were all right."

" Ho ! " said the foreman, shortly ; and just then the eyes of the young men met, and it seemed to Richard that there was written in those of the vicar the one word, " Liar ! "

" Did you speak, sir ? " said Richard, blanching, and then speaking hotly.

" No, Mr. Glaire, I did not speak, but I will, for I should like to say that from what I have seen of that young man Podmore, I do not think he is one who would be guilty of such a dastardly action."

"How can you know?" said Richard, flushing up. "You only came to the town yesterday."

"True," said the vicar; "but this young man was my guide here, and I had some talk with him."

"I hope you did him good," said Richard, with an angry sneer.

"I hope I did, Mr. Glaire," said the vicar, meaningly, "and I think I did, for he told me something of his life, and I gave him some advice."

"Of course," from Richard.

"Richard, my son, pray remember," exclaimed Mrs. Glaire.

"Oh yes, I remember, mother," cried Richard, stung with rage by the doubting way in which his charge had been received; "but it is just as well that Mr. Selwood here should learn at once that he's not coming to Dumford to be master, and do what he likes with people."

"It is far from my wish, Mr. Glaire," said the vicar, with a bright spot burning on each cheek, for he was young and impulsive too, but the spots died out, and he spoke very calmly. "My desire here is to be the counsellor and friend of both master and man—the trusty counsellor and faithful friend. My acquaintance with this young workman Podmore was short, but I gave him a few friendly words on his future action, and the result was that he came and fought for his master like a man when he was in the midst of an angry mob."

"So he did, parson, so he did," said Banks, bluntly.

"And came in a malicious, cowardly way at night to destroy my property," cried Richard.

"Nay, nay, lad, nay," said Banks, sturdily. "Parson's raight. Tom Podmore ain't the lad to do such a cowardly trick, and don't you let it be known as you said it was him."

"Let it be known!" said Richard, grinding his teeth. "Why, I'll set the police after him, and have him transported as an example."

"Nay, nay, lad," said Banks, "wait a bit, and I'll find out who did this. It wasn't Tom Podmore—I'll answer for that."

"Let him prove it, then — and he shall," cried Richard, who hardly believed it himself; but it was so favourable an opportunity for having an enemy on the hip, that he was determined, come what might, not to let it pass.

Five minutes later the parties separated, the works were shut up, and Richard Glaire did not reject the companionship of the vicar and the foreman to his own door, for there were plenty of lowering faces in the street—women's as well as men's; but the party were allowed to pass in sullen silence, for the strikers felt that "the maister" had something now of which to complain, and the better class of workmen were completely taken aback by the wanton destruction of the machinery bands.

CHAPTER XIII.

THE FOREMAN AT HOME.

THERE had been a few words at Joe Banks's plainly-furnished home when he returned the previous night.

Everything looked very snug — the plain, simple furniture shone in the lamplight, and a cosy meal was prepared, with Mrs. Banks—a Daisy of a very ripened nature—sitting busily at work.

" Well, moother," said Banks, as he entered and threw himself into a chair.

" Well, Joe," said Mrs. Banks, without looking up.

" Phee-ew ! " whistled Joe, softly, as he took up the pipe laid ready beside the old, gray, battered, leaden tobacco-box, filled the bowl, and lit up before speaking again, Mrs. Banks meanwhile making a cup of tea for him to have with his supper.

" Why didn't you come home to tea, Joe— didn't you know there was some pig cheer ? "

" Bit of a row up at the works. Didn't you know ? "

" Bless us and save us, no ! " cried Mrs. Banks, nearly dropping the teapot, and hurrying to her husband's side. " You're not hurt, Joe ? "

" Not a bit, lass. Give us a buss."

Mrs. Banks submitted ungraciously to a salute being placed upon her comely cheek, and then, satisfied that no one was hurt, she proceeded to fill up the pot, and resumed her taciturn behaviour.

" Owd woman's a bit popped," said Joe to himself. Then aloud, " Wheer's Daisy ? "

" That's what I want to know," said Mrs. Banks, tartly. " Wheer's Daisy ? There's no keeping the girl at home now-a-days, gadding about."

"Is she up at the House?" said Joe.

"I suppose so," said Mrs. Banks; "and, mark my words, Joe, no good 'll come of it. It's your doing, mind."

"Nonsense, nonsense, old woman. What's put you out? Come, let's have some supper; I'm 'bout pined."

"Then begin," said Mrs. Banks.

"Not wi'out you, my lass," said Joe, winking at the great broad-faced clock, as much as to say, "That'll bring her round."

"I don't want any supper," said Mrs. Banks.

"More don't I, then," said Joe, with a sigh; and he got up, took off his coat, and then began to unlace his stout boots.

"Bless and save the man! wheer are you going?" exclaimed Mrs. Banks.

"Bed," said Joe, shortly. "Tired out."

"What's the use o' me having sausages cooked and hot ready for you if you go on that a way, Joe?"

"I can't eat sausages wi'out a smile wi'

'em for gravy," said Joe, quietly, "and some one to eat one too."

"There, sit down," said Mrs. Banks, pushing her lord roughly into his well-polished Windsor chair. "I don't know what's come to the man."

"Come home straange and hungry," said Joe, smiling; and the next minute, on Mrs. Banks producing a steaming dish of home-made sausages from the oven, Joe began a tremendous onslaught upon them, after helping his wife, and putting a couple of the best on a plate.

"Just put them i' the oven to keep hot for Daisy, wilt ta, my lass?" said Joe.

"She won't want any supper," said Mrs. Banks, tartly, but she placed the plate in the oven all the same, and after pouring out some tea, set the teapot on the hob.

"But she may, my lass, she may," said Joe. "Now, tell us what's wrong," he continued, with his mouth full, after pouring a large steaming cup of tea down his capacious throat.

"Tom Podmore's been here," said Mrs. Banks. "Only just gone. Didn't you meet him?"

"No," said Joe. "Didn't he say nowt about the row?"

"Not a word," said Mrs. Banks, looking up. "Was he in it?"

"Just was," said Joe. "Saved me and the Maister from being knocked to pieces a'most. He's a good plucky chap, is Tom."

"Yes, and nicely he gets treated for it," said Mrs. Banks, hotly.

"Who treats him nicely?" said Joe, with half a slice of bread and butter disappearing.

"You—Daisy—everybody."

"Self included, my lass!" said Joe. "He allus was a favourite of yours."

"Favourite, indeed!" said Mrs. Banks. "Joe, mark my words—It'll come home to Daisy for jilting him as she's done; and, as I told him to-night, he's a great stupid ghipes to mind anything about the wicked, deceitful girl."

"Here, have some more sausage, mother; it's splendid; and don't get running down your own flesh and blood."

"Own flesh and blood!" cried Mrs. Banks. "I'm ashamed of her."

"No, you're not, lass," said Joe, with a broad grin. "Thou'rt as proud of her as a she peacock wi' two tails. Now, lookye here, lass; you've took quite on that Daisy should have Tom. Well, he's a decent young fellow enew, and if she'd liked him I should ha' said nowt against it, but then she didn't."

"She don't know her own mind," said Mrs. Banks.

"Oh yes, she do," said Joe, smiling, "quite well; and so does some one else. The Missus has fun' it out."

"Mrs. Glaire?"

"Yes, the Missus. She sent for me to-day to speak to me about it."

"What, about her boy coming after our Daisy?"

"About Mr. Richard Glaire, maister o' Doomford Foundry, taking a fancy to, and having matrimonial projects with regard to his foreman's daughter," said Joe, pompously.

"Well!" exclaimed Mrs. Banks, eagerly; "and does she like it?"

"Well—er—er—er—she's about for and again it," said Joe, slowly.

"Now that won't do, Joe," exclaimed Mrs. Banks. "You can't deceive me, and I'm not going to be put aside in that way. I know as well as if I'd ha' been theer that she said she didn't like."

"Well, what does it matter about what the women think? Dick—I mean Maister Richard Glaire's hard after her."

"And means to marry her?" said Mrs. Banks.

"Marry her? Of course. Didn't Baxter, of Churley, marry Jane Kemp? Didn't Bill

Bradby, as was wuth fifty thousand, marry
Polly Robinson of Toddlethorpe, and make a
real lady of her, and she wasn't fit to stand
within ten yards o' my Daisy."

"Yes, go on," said Mrs. Banks. "That's
your pride."

"Pride be——blowed, it's only a difference
in money. Richard Glaire's only my old fellow-
workman's son, and Daisy's my daughter, and
I can buy her as many silk frocks, and as many
watches, and chains, and rings as any lady in
the land need have," said Joe, angrily, as he
slapped his pocket. "I ain't gone on saving
for twenty years for nowt. She shan't disgrace
him when they're married."

"Yes, Joe, that's your pride," said Mrs. Banks.

"Go it," said Joe, angrily, "tant away—
tant—tant—tant. I don't keer."

"It's your pride, that's what it is. When
she might marry a decent, honest, true-hearted
lad like Tom, who's worth fifty Richard Glaires
—an insignificant, stuck-up dandy."

"Don't you abuse him whose bread you eat," said Joe.

"I don't," said Mrs. Banks. "It's his mother's and not his. I believe he soon wouldn't have a bit for himself, if it wasn't for you keeping his business together. Always sporting and gambling, and fooling away his money."

"Well, if I keep it together, it's for our bairn, isn't it?" said Joe.

"And he's no better than he should be."

"You let him alone," said Joe, stoutly. "All young men are a bit wild 'fore they're married. I was for one."

"It's a big story, Joe," said Mrs. Banks, indignantly. "You wasn't, or I shouldn't ha' had you."

Joe winked at the clock again, and laughed a little inside as he unbuttoned another button of his vest—the second beginning at the top— to keep count how many cups of tea he had had.

"It's my opinion," said Mrs. Banks, "that—"

"Howd thee tongue, wilt ta?" cried Joe. "Here's the lass."

Daisy entered as he spoke, looking very pale and anxious-eyed, hastened through the kitchen, and went upstairs to take off her hat and jacket.

"Just you make haste down, miss," said Mrs. Banks, tartly.

"I don't want any supper, mother," said the girl, hurriedly.

"Then I want thee to ha'e some!" exclaimed Mrs. Banks; "so look sharp."

Daisy gave a sigh and hurried upstairs, and, as the door closed, Joe brought his hand down on the table with a thump that made the cups and saucers dance.

"Now, look here, old woman — that's my bairn, and I wean't have her wherrited. If she is——"

"I'm going to say what's on my mind, Joe, when it's for my child's good," said Mrs. Banks, stoutly.

"Are you?" said Joe, taking another cup of tea and undoing another button; "then so am I. Lookye here, my lass! I wouldn't ha' took a step to throw Daisy in young Maister's way, but as he's took to her, why, I wean't ha' it interfered wi'—so now, then."

"Don't blame me, then, Joe; that's all," said Mrs. Banks.

"Who's going to?" said Joe. "So now let's have none of your clat."

Daisy came in then, and took her place at the table, making a very sorry pretence at eating, and only speaking in monosyllables till her mother pressed her.

"Did Mrs. Glaire send you home with anybody?"

"No, mother."

"Did you come home alone?"

"No, mother."

"Humph: who came with you?"

"Tom, mother."

Mrs. Banks looked mollified, and Joe surprised.

"Has Miss Eve been playing to you, to-night?"

"No, mother."

"What have you been doing then?"

"I—I—haven't been at the House," stammered Daisy.

Joe turned sharply round.

"Have you been a-walking with Tom, then?"

"No, mother, I only met him — coming home—and he walked beside me," said the girl, with crimson cheeks.

"Theer, theer, theer," said Joe, interposing, "let the bairn alone. Daisy, my lass, mak' me a round o' toast."

How Joe was going to dispose of a round of toast after the meal he had already devoured was a problem; but Daisy darted a grateful look at him, made the toast—which was not eaten—and then, after the things were cleared away, read for an hour to her father, straight up and down the columns of the week-old county paper, till it was time for bed, without a single interruption.

But Mrs. Banks made up for it when they went to bed, and the last words Joe heard before going to sleep were—

" Well, Joe, I wash my hands of the affair. It's your doing, and she's your own bairn."

And Joe Banks went to sleep, and dreamed of seeing himself in a new suit of clothes, throwing an old shoe after Daisy as she was being carried off by Richard Glaire in a carriage drawn by four gray horses, the excitement being such that he awoke himself in the act of crying " Hooray!" while poor Daisy was kneeling by her bedside, sobbing as though she would break her heart.

CHAPTER XIV.

SIM SLEE SEES ANOTHER OPENING.

"Here, just hap me up a bit," said Sim
Slee to his wife, as he lay down on a rough
kind of couch in their little keeping-room, as
the half sitting-room, half kitchen was called;
and in obedience to the command, Mrs. Slee
happed him up—in other words, threw a patch-
work counterpane over her lord.

"If you'd come home at reasonable times
and tak' thee rest you wouldn't be wantin' to
sleep in the middle o' the day," said Mrs. Slee,
roughly.

"Ah, a deal you know about things,"
grumbled Sim. "You'd see me starved with
cold before you'd stir, when I was busy half
the night over the affairs of the town."

"I'stead o' your own," grumbled Mrs. Slee.

"Howd thee tongue, woman," said Sim. "I'm not going to sleep, but to think over matters before I go and see Joe Banks this afternoon. I can think best lying down."

Mrs. Slee resumed her work, which was that of making a hearthrug of shreds of cloth, and soon after Sim was thinking deeply with his mouth open, and his breath coming and going with an unpleasant gurgle.

As soon as he was asleep, Mrs. Slee began busily to prepare the humble dinner that was cooking, and spread the clean white table for her lord's meal. A table-cloth was a luxury undreamed of, but on so white a table it did not seem necessary.

When all was ready, she went across the room and touched Sim, who opened his eyes and rose.

"That's better," he said. "I feel as tiff as a band now. Where's the Rag Jack's oil?"

Without a word, Mrs. Slee went to a little

cupboard and produced a dirty-looking bottle of the unpleasant-looking liquid, one which was looked upon in the district as an infallible cure for every kind of injury, from cuts and bruises down to chilblains, and the many ailments of the skin.

"How did you do that?" said Mrs. Slee, sharply, as her husband held out a finger that was torn and evidently festering.

"Somebody was nation fast the other day, and pulled me off the foundry wall."

"Where you'd got up to speak, eh?" said Mrs. Slee.

"Where I'd got up to speak," said Sim, holding his hand, while his wife dressed it with the balm composed by the celebrated Rag Jack, a dealer who went round from market to market, and then tied it up in a bit of clean linen.

"That's better," said Sim, taking his place at the table. "What is there to yeat?"

"There'd be nothing if it was left to you—

but wind," said his wife, sourly, as she took the lid off a boiler, hanging from the recking-hooks of the galley balk, and proceeded to take out some liquid with a tea-cup.

"But, then, it ain't," said Sim, smiling. "You see, I knew where to pick up a good missus."

"Yes," retorted his wife, "and then tried to pine her to dead for all you'd do to feed her. Will ta have a few broth?"

"Yes," said Sim, taking the basin she offered him and sniffing at it. "Say, wife, you've been waring your money at a pretty rate."

"I've wared no money ower that," said Mrs. Slee. "Thou mayst thank parson for it."

"Yah!" growled Sim, dipping his spoon, and beginning angrily; "this mutton's as tough as a bont whong."

"There, do sup thee broth like a Christian, if thee canst!" exclaimed Mrs. Slee. "Wilt ta have a tate?"

Sim held out his basin for the "tate" his

wife was denuding of its jacket, and she dropped it into the broth.

"Say!" exclaimed Sim, poking at the potato with his spoon, "these taters are strange and sad."

Mrs. Slee did not make any reply, but went on peeling potatoes one by one, evidently in search of a floury one to suit her husband, who objected to those of a waxy or "sad" nature. But they were all alike, and he had to be content.

"I'll have a few more broth," said Sim, at the end of a short space of time, and before his wife had had an opportunity to partake of a mouthful; and this being ladled out for him and finished, Sim condescended to say "that them broth wasn't bad."

"Have you got any black beer?" he now asked.

Mrs. Slee had—a little, and the bottle of black beer, otherwise spruce, being produced, Sim had a teaspoonful of the treacly fluid mixed in a mug of hot water with a little sugar; and then, leaving his wife to have her meal, he rose and went out.

A week had passed since the discovery of the loss of the bands, and though Sim had been dodging about and watching in all directions, he had never once hit upon Joe Banks alone, so he had at last made up his mind to go straight to his house, and, to use his own words, " beard the lion in his den."

A good deal had taken place in the interval, and among other things, Richard Glaire, in opposition to the advice of his mother and Banks, had applied for a warrant against Tom Podmore, for destroying or stealing the bands; but as yet, from supineness or fear on the part of the local police, it had not been put in force·

For things did not look pleasant in Dumford; men were always standing about in knots or lounging at the doors of their houses, looking loweringly at people who passed. There had been no violence, and, in a prosperous little community, a week or two out of work had little effect upon a people of naturally saving habits and considerable industry; but those who were wise in such matters said that mischief was brewing, and it was reported that meetings were held nightly at the Bull and Cucumber—meetings of great mystery, where oaths were taken, and where the doors were closed and said to be guarded by men with drawn swords.

"Hallo, Sim Slee, off preaching somewhere?" said a very stout man, pulling up his horse as he overtook Sim on his way to the foreman's house. He was indeed a very stout man, so stout that he completely filled the gig from side to side, making its springs collapse, and forming a heavy load for his well-fed horse.

"No, I ain't going preaching nowheer, Mester Purley," said Sim, sulkily, as he looked up sidewise in the speaker's merry face.

"I thought you were off perhaps to a camp meeting, or something, Sim, and as I'm going out as far as Roby, I was going to offer you a lift along the road."

There was a twinkle in the stout man's eyes as he spoke, and he evidently enjoyed the joke.

" No, you warn't going to offer me a ride, doctor," said Sim. " Do you think I don't know ?"

" Right, Sim Slee, right," said the doctor, chuckling. " I never gave a man a lift on the road in my life, did I, Sim ? Puzzle any one to sit by my side here, wouldn't it ?"

" Strange tight fit for him if he did," said Sim.

" So it would, Sim; so it would, Sim," laughed the doctor. " I've asked a many though in my time ; ha—ha—ha."

" That you have, doctor," said Sim, looking at the goodly proportions of the man by his side. For it was Mr.—otherwise Dr.—Purley's one joke to ask everybody he overtook, or any of his convalescent patients, if they would have a lift in his gig. He had probably fired

the joke as many times as he was days old;
but it was always in use, and it never struck
him that it might grow stale.

" What's the matter with your hand, Sim ?"
said the doctor, touching the bound-up member
with his whip.

" Bit hurt—fell off a wall," said Sim, thrusting it in his breast.

" And you have been poisoning it with Rag
Jack oil, eh ? I'll be bound you have, and
when it's down bad you'll come to me to cure
it. Say, Sim, some of your fellows knocked
the young master about pretty well—he's rare
and bruised."

" I wish ivery bit of gruzzle in his body was
bruzz," said Sim, fiercely.

" Do you now !" said the doctor, smiling.
" Well, I suppose it'll come to broken heads
with some of you, and then you'll be glad of
me. Who stole the bands ?"

Sim jumped and turned pale, so suddenly
and sharply was the question asked.

" How should I know ? " he cried, recovering himself.

" Some of you chaps at the Bull, eh, Sim ? Artful trick, very.   Say, Sim, if you want a doctor for your society, remember me.   Ck ! "

This last was to the horse, which went off immediately at a sharp trot, with the springs of the gig dancing up and down, as the wheels went in and out of the ruts.

" Remember you, eh ! " said Sim, as the doctor went out of hearing.   " Have you for the medical man ?   Yes, when we want ivery word as is spoke blabbed all over the place. It's my belief," continued Sim, sententiously, " as that fat old blobkite tells the last bit o' news, to every baby as soon as it's born, and asks them as he's killed whether they'd like a ride in his gig.   Hallo ! there's owd Joe Banks leaning over his fence.   What a fierce-looking old maulkin he is ; he looks as sour as if he'd been yeating berry pie wi'out sugar.   Day, Banks," he said, stopping.

"Day," said Joe, shortly, and staring very hard at the visitor.

"I think it'll rean soon, mun."

"Do yow?" said Joe, roughly

"I weer over to Churley yesterday," said Sim, "and it reant all day."

"Did it?" said Joe.

"Ay, it did. 'Twas a straange wet day."

"Where are you going?" said Joe.

"Oh, only just up to Brown's to see if I could buy a bit o' kindling for the Missus."

"Go and buy it, then," said Joe, turning his back, "and let me get shut o' thee."

"Say, Joe Banks," said Sim, quite unabashed, "as I have met thee I should just like to say a word or two to thee."

"Say away then."

"Nay, nay. Not here. Say, mun, that's a fine primp hedge o' yourn," he continued, pointing to the luxuriant privet hedge that divided the garden of the snug house from the road.

"You let my primp hedge bide," said Joe, sharply; "and if you've got any mander o' message from your lot, spit it out like a man."

"Message! I a message!" said Sim, with a surprised air. "Not I. It was a word or two 'bout thy lass."

Joe Banks's face became crimson, and he turned sharply to see if any one was at door or window so as to have overheard Sim's words.

As there was no one, he came out of the gate, took his caller's arm firmly in his great fist, and walked with him down the lane out of sight of the houses, for the foreman's pretty little place was just at the edge of the town, and looked right down the valley.

Sim's heart beat a little more quickly, and he felt anything but comfortable; but, calling up such determination as he possessed, he walked on till Joe stopped short, faced him, and then held up a menacing finger.

"Now look here, Sim Slee," said Joe; "I

just warn thee to be keerful, for I'm in no humour to be played wi'."

"Who wants to play wi' you?" said Sim; "I just come in a neighbourly way to gi'e ye a bit o' advice, and you fly at me like a lion."

"Thou'rt no neighbour o' mine," said Joe, "and thou'rt come o' no friendly errant. Yow say yow want to speak to me 'bout my lass. Say thee say."

"Oh, if that's the way you tak' it," said Sim, "I'm going."

"Nay, lad, thee ain't," said Joe. "Say what thee've got to say now, for not a step do yow stir till yo' have."

Sim began to repent his visit; but seeing no way of escape, and his invention providing him with no inoffensive tale, he began at once, making at the same time a good deal of show of his bound-up hand, and wincing and nursing it as if in pain.

"Well, Joe Banks, as a man for whom, though we have differed in politics and matters connected with the wucks, I always felt a great respect——"

"Dal thee respect!" said Joe; "come to the point, man."

"I say, Joe, that it grieves me to see thee stick so to a mester as is trying to do thee an injury."

"An yow want to talk me over to join thy set o' plotting, conspiring shackbags at the Bull, eh?"

"I should be straange and proud to feel as I'd browt a man o' Joe Banks's power and common sense into the ways o' wisdom, and propose him as a member o' our society," said Sim.

"I dare say thee would, Sim; strange and glad. But that's not what thee come to say. Out wi' it, mun; out wi' it."

"That is what I come to say, Joe," said Sim, turning white, as he saw the fierce look in Joe's eyes.

"Nay; thee said something 'bout my lass."

"I only were going to say as I didn't like to see such a worthy man serving faithful a mester as was trying to do him an injury."

"What do you mean?" said Joe, quite calmly.

Sim hesitated, but he felt obliged to speak, so calmly firm was the look fixed upon him, though at the same time the foreman's fists were clenched most ominously.

"Well, Joe," said Sim, with a burst, "Dicky Glaire's allus after thy bairn, and I saw him the other night, at nearly midnight, trying to drag her into the counting-house."

"Thee lies, thee chattering, false-hearted maulkin!" roared Joe, taking the trembling man by the throat and shaking him till his teeth clicked together.

"Don't! don't! murder!" cried Sim, holding up his injured hand with the rag before Joe's face. "Don't ill-use a helpless man."

"Thou chattering magpie!" roared Joe, throwing him off, so that Sim staggered back against the prickly hedge, and quickly started upright. "I wish thee weer a man that I could thrash till all thee bones was sore. Look here, Sim Slee, if thee says a word again about my lass and the doings of thee betters it'll be the worse for thee."

"My poor hand! my poor hand!" moaned Sim, nursing it as if it were seriously injured.

"Then thee shouldn't ha' made me wroth," said Joe, calming down, and blaming himself for attacking a cripple.

"I didn't know that thou wast going to wink at thee lass being Dicky Glaire's mis——"

Sim did not finish the word, for Joe Banks's fist fell upon his mouth with a heavy thud, and he went down in the road, and lay there with his lips bleeding, and a couple of his front teeth loosened.

"Thou lying villin," said Joe, hoarsely, "howd thee tongue, if thee wants to stay me from killing thee. I'd ha' let thee off, but

thou wouldst hev it.   Don't speak to me
again, or I shall——"

He did not trust himself to finish, but strode
off, leaving Slee lying in the dust.

"Poor Master Richard," he muttered—"a
scandal-hatching, lying scoundrel — as if the
lad would think a wrong word about my lass.
Well," he added, with a forced laugh, "that
has stopped his mouth, and a good many more,
as I expect."

As he disappeared, Sim Slee slowly sat up,
took out his handkerchief and wiped his bleeding mouth.   Then rising he walked on half a
mile to where a stream, known as the Beck,
crossed the road, and there he stooped down
and bathed his cut lip till the bleeding ceased.

"All raight, Mester Joe Banks," he said, with
a malicious look in his eye.   "All raight, I'll
put that down to you, my lad.   I shan't forget
it.   Some men fights wi' their fists, and some
don't.   I'm one as don't; but I can fight other
ways.   I'll be even wi' you, Joe Banks; I'll

be even wi' you. Thou blind owd bat. Think
he'll marry her, dosta! Ha! ha! ha! ha!
All raight. Let it go on. Suppose I help it
now, and then get thee on our side after—a
blind old fool, I shan't forget this."

Sim Slee washed his handkerchief carefully
in the brook, spread it in the sun to dry, and
then lay down amongst the furze bushes to
think, till, seeing a couple of figures in the
distance on the hill-side, he caught up his
handkerchief and, stooping down, ran along
under the shelter of the hedge, and on and on
till he reached a fir plantation, through which
he made his way till he was within easy reach
of the two figures, in utter ignorance of his
proximity.

" 'Tis them," he muttered, peering out from
the screen of leaves formed by the undergrowth
of the edge of the plantation. " 'Tis them.
Got his arm round her waist, eh! A kiss, eh!
Ha—ha—ha! Joe Banks, I shall be upsides
wi' you yet."

He glided back, and then, knowing every inch of the ground, he went to the end of the copse, out on to the open hill-side, and, running fast, made a circuit which brought him out on the track far beyond the figures, who were hidden from him by the inequalities of the waste land, close by where the vicar found Tom Podmore on his arrival.

Then, hastening on, he approached, stooping until he had well measured his distance, when, pausing for a few minutes to gain his breath, he walked on with his footsteps inaudible on the soft, velvety turf, till, coming suddenly upon the two figures, seated behind a huge block of stone, he stopped short, as if in surprise.

" Beg pardon, sir, didn't see," he said, with a smile and a leer.

"What the deuce do you want?" said Richard Glaire, starting to his feet, while, with a faint cry, Daisy Banks ran a few steps.

" Why you quite scar'd me, sir," said Sim,

"starting up like that. I've only been for a walk out Chorley way. It's all raight, Miss Banks, don't be scar'd; it's only me. I know, Mr. Glaire, sir, I know. Young folks and all that sort o' thing. We ain't friends about wuck matters, but you may trust me."

He gave Richard a peculiar smile, shut one eye slowly, and walked on, smiling at Daisy, whose face was crimson as he passed.

"Oh, Richard! oh, Richard!" she sobbed, "why did you tempt me to come? Now he'll go straight home and tell father."

"Tempt you to come, eh, Daisy!" said Richard. "Why, because I love you so; I'm not happy out of your sight. No, he won't tell—a scoundrel. There, you go home the other way. I'll follow Master Sim Slee. I know the way to seal up his lips."

He caught Daisy in his arms, and kissed her twice before she could evade his grasp, and then ran off after Slee, who was steadily walking on, smiling, as he caressed his tender, bruised lip with his damp handkerchief.

Once he pressed his thumb down on his palm in a meaning way, and gave an ugly wink. Then he chuckled, but checked his smiles, for they hurt his swollen face.

"Not bad for one day, eh! That's ointment for Mester Joe Banks's sore place, and a bit o' revenge at the same time. This wean't have nowt to do wi' the strike; this is all private. Here he comes," he muttered, twitching his ears. "I thowt he would. Well, I mean to hev five pun' to howd my tongue, and more when I want it. And mebbe," he continued, with an ugly leer, "I can be a bit useful to him now and then."

A minute later Richard Glaire had overtaken Sim Slee, and a short conversation ensued, in the course of which something was thrust into the schemer's hand. Then they parted, and that night, in spite of his swollen lip, Sim Slee delivered a wonderful oration on

the rights of the British workman at the meeting at the Bull, at which were present several
of the men after Sim's own heart; but the
shrewd, sensible workmen were conspicuous by
their absence, as they were having a quiet
meeting of their own.

CHAPTER XV.

DAISY IS OBSTINATE.

" A LUNGEING villain," muttered Joe Banks to himself, "he knows nowt but nastiness. Strange thing that a man can't make up to a pretty girl wi'out people putting all sorts o' bad constructions on it. Why they're all alike —Missis Glaire, the wife and all. My Daisy, too. To say such a word of her."

He hastened home, filled his pipe, lit it, and went out and sat down in the garden, in front of his bees, to smoke and watch them, while he calmed himself down and went over what had gone by, before thinking over the future.

This was a favourite place with Joe Banks on a Sunday, and he would sit in contempla- tive study here for hours. For he said it was

like having a holiday and looking at somebody
else work, especially when the bees were busy
in the glass bells turned over the flat-topped
hives.

"I'd no business to hit a crippled man like
that," mused Joe; "but he'd no business to
anger me. Be a lesson to him."

He filled a fresh pipe, lit it by holding the
match sheltered in his hands, and then went
on—

"Be a lesson to him—a hard one, for my
hand ain't light. Pity he hadn't coot away,
for he put me out."

"Now, what'll I do?" mused Joe. "Shall
I speak to the maister?

"No, I wean't. He'll speak to me when it's
all raight, and Daisy and him has made it up.
I'll troost him, that I will; for though he's a
bit wild, he's a gentleman at heart, like his
father before him. Why of course I'll troost
him. He's a bit shamefaced about it o' course;
but he'll speak all in good time. Both of 'em

will, and think they're going to surprise me.
Ha—ha—ha! I've gotten 'em though. Lord,
what fools young people is—blind as bats—
blind as bats. Here's Daisy."

"It's so nice to see you sitting here, father,"
said the girl, coming behind him, and resting
her chin on his bald crown, while her plump
arms went round his neck.

"Is it, my gal? That's raight. Why,
Daisy lass, what soft little arms thine are.
Give us a kiss."

Daisy leaned down and kissed him, and then
stopped with her arms resting on his shoulders,
keeping her face from confronting him; and so
they remained for a few minutes, when a smile
twinkled about the corners of the foreman's
lips and eyes as he said—

"Daisy, my gal, I've been watching the bees
a bit."

"Yes, father," she said, smiling, though it
was plain to see that the smile was forced.
"Yes, father, you always like to watch the bees."

"I do, my bairn, I do. They're just like so many workmen in a factory; but they don't strike, my gal, they don't strike."

"But they swarm, father," said Daisy, making an effort to keep up the conversation.

"Yes," chuckled Joe, taking hold of the hand that rested on his left shoulder. "Yes, my bairn, I was just coming to that. They swarm, don't they?"

"Yes, father."

"And do you know why they swarm, Daisy?"

"Yes, father; because the hive is not big enough for them."

"Yes, yes," chuckled Joe, patting the hand, and holding it to his rough cheek. "You're raight, but it's something more, Daisy: it's the young ones going away from home and setting up for theirselves—all the young ones 'most do that some day."

The tears rose to Daisy's eyes, and she tried to withdraw her hand, for Joe had touched on a tenderer point than he imagined; but he held it tightly and gave it a kiss.

"There, there, my pet," he said, tenderly, "I won't tease you. I knew it would come some day all right enough, and I don't mind. I only want my little lass to be happy."

"Oh, father—father—father," sobbed Daisy, letting her face droop till it rested on his head, while her tears fell fast.

"Come, come, come, little woman," he said, laughing; "thou mustn't cry. Why, it's all raight." There was a huskiness in his voice though, as he spoke, and he had to fight hard to make the dew disappear from his eyes. "Here, I say, Daisy, my lass, that wean't do no good: you may rain watter for ever on my owd bald head, and the hair won't come again. There — tut — tut — tut — you'll have moother here directly, and she'll be asking what's wrong."

Daisy made a strong effort over self, and succeeded at last in drying her eyes.

"Then, you are not cross with me, father?" faltered Daisy.

"Cross, my darling? not a bit," said Joe, patting her hand again. "You shan't disgrace the man as has you, my dear; that you shan't. Why, you're fit to be a little queen, you are."

Daisy gave him a hasty kiss, and ran off, while Joe proceeded to refill his pipe.

"Cross indeed! I should just think I hadn't," he exclaimed—"only with the women. Well, they'll come round."

But if Joe Banks had stood on the hill-side a couple of hours earlier, just by the spot where Tom Podmore had sat on the day of the vicar's arrival, he would perhaps have viewed the matter in a different light, for—of course by accident—Daisy had there encountered Richard Glaire, evidently not for the first time since the night when they were interrupted by Tom in the lane.

It was plain that any offence Richard had given on the night in question had long been condoned, and that at every meeting he was gaining a stronger mastery over the girl's heart.

"Then you will, Daisy, won't you?" he whispered to her.

"No, no, Dick dear. Don't ask me. Let me tell father all about it."

"What?" he cried.

"Let me tell father all about it, and I'm sure he'll be pleased."

"My dear little Daisy, how well you are named," he cried, playfully; and as he looked lovingly down upon her, the foolish girl began to compare him with the lover of her mother's choice—a man who was nearly always blackened with his labours, and heavy and rough spoken, while here was Richard Glaire professing that he worshipped her, and looking, in her eyes, so handsome in his fashionably-cut blue coat with the rosebud in the button-hole, and wearing patent leather boots as tight as the lemon gloves upon his well-formed hands.

"I can't help my name," she said, coquettishly.

"I wouldn't have it changed for the world, my little pet," he whispered, playing with her dimpled chin; "only you are as fresh as a daisy."

"What do you mean, Dick?" she said, nestling to him.

"Why you are so young and innocent. Look here, my darling: don't you see how I'm placed? My mother wants me to marry Eve."

"But you don't really, really, really, care the least little bit for her, do you, Mr. Richard?"

"'Mr. Richard!'" reproachfully.

"Dear Dick, then," she whispered, colouring up, and glancing fondly at him, half ashamed though the while at her boldness.

"Of course I don't love her. Haven't I sworn a hundred times that I love only you, and that I want you to be my darling little wife?"

"Yes, yes," said the girl, softly.

"Well, then, my darling, if you go and tell your father, the first thing he'll do will be to go and tell my mother, and then there'll be no end of a row."

"But she loves you very much, Dick."

"Worships me," said Dick, complacently.

"Of course," said the girl, softly; and her foolish little eyes seemed to say, "She couldn't help it," while she continued, "and she'd let you do as you like, Dick."

"Well, but you see the devil of it is, Daisy, that I promised her I wouldn't see you any more."

"Why did you do that?" said the girl, sharply.

"To save rows—I hate a bother."

"Richard, you were ashamed of me, and wouldn't own me," said Daisy, bursting into tears.

"Oh, what a silly, hard-hearted, cruel little blossom it is," said Richard, trying to console her, but only to be pushed away. "All I did and said was to save bother, and not upset the old girl. That's why I want it all kept quiet. Here, as I tell you, I could be waiting for you over at Chorley, we could pop into the mail as it came through, off up to London, be married by licence, and then the old folks would be in a bit of a temper for a week, and as pleased as Punch afterwards."

"Oh, no, Richard, I couldn't, couldn't do that," said the girl, panting with excitement.

"Yes, you could," he said, "and come back after a trip to Paris, eh, Daisy? where you should have the run of the fashions. What would they all say when you came back a regular lady, and I took you to the house?"

"Oh, Dick, dear Dick, don't ask me," moaned the poor girl, whose young head was in a whirl. "I couldn't—indeed I couldn't be so wicked."

"So wicked! no, of course not," said Richard, derisively—"a wicked little creature. Oh, dear, what would become of you if you married Richard Glaire!"

"You're teasing me," she said, "and it's very cruel of you."

"Horribly," said Richard. "But you will come, Daisy?"

"I couldn't, I couldn't," faltered the girl.

"Yes, you could, you little goose."

"Dick, my own handsome, brave Dick," she whispered, "let me tell father."

He drew back from her coldly.

"You want to be very obedient, don't you?"

"Oh, yes, dear Richard," she said, looking at him appealingly.

"You set such a good example, Daisy, that I must be very good too."

"Yes, dear," she said, innocently.

"Yes," he said, with a sneer; "so you go and tell your father like a good little child, and I'll be a good boy, too, and go and tell my mother, and she'll scold me and say I've been very naughty, and make me marry Eve."

"Oh, Richard, Richard, how can you be so cruel?" cried the poor girl, reproachfully.

" It isn't I ; it's you," he said, smiling with satisfaction as he saw what a plaything the girl's heart was in his hands. " Are you going to tell your father ? "

"'Oh, no, Dick, not if you say I mustn't."

" Well, that's what I do say," he exclaimed sharply.

" Very well, Dick," she said, sadly.

" And look here, Daisy, my own little one," he whispered, kissing her tear-wet face, " some day, when I ask you, it shall be as I say, eh ? "

" Oh, Dick, darling, I'll do anything you wish but that. Don't ask me to run away."

" Do you want to break off our match ? " he said, bitterly.

" Oh, no—no—no—no."

" Do you want to make my home miserable ? "

" You know I don't, Richard."

" Because, I tell you I know my mother will never consent to it unless she is forced."

"But you are your own master now, Richard," she pleaded.

"Not so much as you think for, my little woman. So come, promise me. I know you won't break your word if you do promise."

"No, Dick, never," she said, earnestly; and if there had been any true love in the young fellow's breast he would have been touched by the trusting, earnest reliance upon him that shone from her eyes as she looked up affectionately in his face.

"Then promise me, Daisy, dear," he whispered; "it is for the good of both of us, and—— Hang it all, there's Slee."

Daisy was sent off as we know, and the tears fell fast as she hastened home, feeling that love was very sweet, but that its roses had thorns that rankled and stung.

"Oh, Dick, Dick," she sobbed as she went on, "I wish sometimes that I'd never seen you, for it is so hard not to do whatever you wish."

She dried her eyes hastily as she neared

home, and drew her breath a little more hardly as about a hundred yards from the gate she saw Tom Podmore, who looked at her firmly and steadily as they passed, and hardly responded to her nod.

"He knows where I've been. He knows where I've been," whispered Daisy to herself as she hurried on ; and she was quite right, for her conscious cheeks hoisted a couple of signal flags of the ruddiest hue—signals that poor Tom could read as well as if they had been written down in a code, and he ground his teeth as he turned and watched her.

"She's such a good girl that any one might troost her," he muttered, as he saw her go in at the gate, "or else I'd go and tell Joe all as I knows. But no, I couldn't do that, for it would hurt her, just as it would if I was to half kill Dick Glaire. She'll find him out some day perhaps—not as it matters to me though, for it's all over now."

He walked back, looking over the green fence

as he passed, and Mrs. Banks waved her hand to him from the window; but his eyes were too much occupied by the sight of Daisy leaning over her father, and he walked on so hurriedly that he nearly blundered up against a great stalwart figure coming the other way.

CHAPTER XVI.

THE VICAR'S FRIENDS.

" What cheer, owd Tommy?" cried the stalwart figure, pulling a short black pipe out of his mouth.

" Hallo, Harry," said Tom, quietly, at least as quietly as he could, for the words were jerked out of his mouth by the tremendous clap on the shoulder administered by the big hammerman.

" What's going to be done, Tommy?" growled the great fellow. " I'm 'bout tired o' this. I wants to hit something."

He stretched out his great sinewy arm, and then drawing it back, let it fly again with such force that a man would have gone down before it like a cork.

"Come along," said Tom, who wished to get away from the neighbourhood of Banks's cottage for fear Mrs. Banks should call to him.

Harry was a man whose brain detested originality. He was a machine who liked to be set in motion, so he followed Tom like a huge dog, and without a word.

As they came abreast of the vicarage they saw the vicar at work gardening, and Jacky Budd making believe to dig very hard in the wilderness still unreclaimed.

Even at their distance, Jacky's pasty face and red ripe nose, suggestive of inward tillage, were plainly to be seen, and just then a thought seemed to strike Tom, who turned to his companion, staring with open mouth over the hedge.

"Like a job, Harry?"

"Hey, lad, I should."

"Come in here then," said Tom, laying his hand on the gate.

"That I will, lad," said Harry. "I want to scrarp some un, and I should 'mazin like a fail wi' that theer parson."

Tom smiled grimly, and entered, followed by Harry.

They were seen directly by the vicar, who came up and shook hands with Tom.

"Ah, Podmore, glad to see you. Well, Harry, my man," he continued, holding out his hand to the other, "is the lump on your forehead gone?"

Harry took the vicar's hand and held it in a mighty grip, while with his left he removed his cap and looked in the lining, as if to see if the bruise was there.

"Never thowt no more 'bout it, parson." Then gazing down at the soft hand he held, he muttered, "It's amaazin'!"

"What's amazing?" said the vicar, smiling.

"Why that you could hit a man such a crack wi' a hand like this 'ere."

"Don't mind him, sir; it's his way," said

Tom, apologetically. "Fact is, parson, we're tired o' doing nowt."

"I'm glad to hear you say so, Podmore," said the vicar, earnestly. "I wish from my heart this unhappy strife were at an end. I'm trying my best."

"Of course you are, sir," said Tom; "but I thowt mebbe you'd give Harry here and me a bit o' work."

"Work! what work?" said the vicar, wonderingly.

"Well, you said I'd best get to work, and I've got nowt to do. That Jacky Budd there's picking about as if he was scarred o' hurting the ground: let me and Harry dig it up."

The vicar looked from one to the other for a moment, and as his eyes rested on Harry, that giant gave Tom a clap on the shoulder hard enough to make a bruise, as he exclaimed—

"Hark at that now, for a good'n, parson. Here, gie's hold of a shovel."

The vicar led the way to the tool-house, fur-

nished his visitors with tools, and then stood
close at hand to supply the science, while the
way in which the two men began to dig had
such an effect on Jacky Budd that he stood
still and perspired.

A dozen great shovelfuls of earth were turned
over by Harry, who then stopped short, threw
off his coat and vest, tightened the belt round
his waist, and loosening the collar of his shirt,
proceeded to roll up the sleeves before moisten-
ing his hands and seizing the spade once more,
laughing heartily as he turned over the soft
earth like a steam plough.

"Slip int' it, Tommy. Well, this is a game.
It's straange and fine though, after doin' nowt
for a week."

Tom was digging steadily and well, for he
was a bit of a gardener in his way, having often
helped Joe Banks to dig his piece in the early
days of his love.

"Better borry some more garden, parson;
we shall ha' done this 'ere in 'bout an hour and

a half," said Harry, grinning; and then —— crack !

"Look at that for a tool!" he cried, holding up the broken shovel, snapped in two at the handle.

"Try this one, Harry," said Jacky Budd, handing his own spade eagerly; "I've got some hoeing to do."

Harry took the tool and worked away a little more steadily, with the result that poor Jacky Budd was deprived of a good deal of the work that would have fallen to his lot; a deprivation, however, that he suffered without a sigh.

"Now, I ain't agoing to beg, parson," said Harry, after a couple of hours' work, "but my forge wants coal, and a bite o' bread and a bit o' slip-coat cheese would be to raights."

"Slip-coat cheese ?" said the vicar.

"He means cream cheese," said Tom, who had been working away without a word, keeping Jacky busy clearing away the weeds.

"No, I don't," growled Harry. "I mean slip-coat, and a moog o' ale."

"Shall I go and fetch some, sir?" said Jacky Budd, eagerly.

"Thank you, no, Budd," said the vicar, quietly. "I won't take you from your work;" and, to Jacky's great disgust, he went and fetched a jug of ale from his little cellar himself.

"He ain't a bad un," cried Harry, tearing away at the earth. "Keeps a drink o' ale i' the plaace. I thowt parsons allus drunk port wine."

"Not always, my man," said the vicar, handing the great fellow the jug, and while he was drinking, up came Jacky with his lips parted, and a general look on his visage as if he would like to hang his tongue out like a thirsty hound and pant.

"Shall I get the leather, sir, and just nail up that there bit o' vine over the window?"

"Get the what, Budd?" said the vicar, who looked puzzled.

" The leather, sir, the leather."

" He means the lather, sir," said Tom, quietly, " the lather to climb up."

" Oh, the ladder," said the vicar. " Yes, by all means," he continued, smiling as he saw the clerk's thirsty look. " I won't ask you to drink, Budd," he went on as he handed the mug to Tom, who took a hearty draught. " You told me you did not drink beer on principle; and I never like to interfere with a man's principles, though I hold that beer in moderation is good for out-door workers."

" Thanky, sir, quite right, sir," said Jacky, with a blank look on his face. " I'll get the leather and a few nails, and do that vine now."

" Poof!" ejaculated Harry, with a tremendous burst of laughter, as he went on digging furiously. " Well, that's alarming."

" What's the matter, old mate?" said Tom.

" Nowt at all. Poof!" he roared again, turning over the earth. " Jacky Budd don't drink beer ou principle. Poof!"

The vicar paid no heed to him, only smiled to himself, and the gardening progressed at such a rate that by five o'clock what had been a wilderness began to wear a very pleasant aspect of freedom from weeds and overgrowth, and with the understanding that the two workers were to come and finish in the morning, they resumed their jackets and went off.

Their visit to the vicarage had not passed unnoticed, however; for Sim Slee had been hanging about, seeking for an opportunity to have a word with his wife, and not seeing her, he had carried the news to the Bull and Cucumber.

"Things is coming to a pretty pass," he said to the landlord. "That parson's got a way of getting ower iverybody. What do you think now?"

"Can't say," said the landlord.

"He's gotten big Harry and Tom Podmore working in his garden like two big beasts at plough."

"He'll be gettin' o' you next, Sim," said the landlord, laughing.

"Gettin' o' me!" echoed Sim. "Not he. He tried it on wi' me as soon as we met; but I wrastled with him by word o' mouth, and he went down like a stone."

"Did he though, Sim?"

"Ay, lad. Yon parson's all very well, but he's fra London, and he'll hev to get up pretty early to get over a Lincoln man, eh?"

"Ay," said the landlord; "but he ain't so bad nayther. A came here and sat down just like a christian, and talked to the missus and played wi' the bairns for long enough."

"Did he though," said Sim. "Hey, lad, but that's his artfulness. He wants to get the whip hand o' thee."

"I dunno 'bout that," said the landlord, who eked out his income from the publican business with a little farming. "I thowt so at first, and expected he'd want to read a chapter and give me some tracks."

"Well, didn't he?" said Sim.

"Nay, not he. We only talked once 'bout 'ligious matters, and 'bout the chapel—ay, and we talked 'bout you an' all."

"'Bout me?" said Sim, getting interested, and pausing with his mug half way to his lips.

"Yes," said the landlord. "It come about throof me saying I see he'd gotten your missus to keep house for him."

"Give me another gill o' ale," said Sim, now deeply interested.

The landlord filled his mug for him, and went on—

"I said she were 'bout the cleanest woman in these parts, and the way she'd fettle up a place and side things was wonderful."

"Yow needn't ha' been so nation fast talking 'bout my wife," said Sim.

"I niver said nowt agen her," said the landlord, chuckling to himself. "And then we got talking 'bout you and the chapel."

"What did he know 'bout me and the chapel?" cried Sim, angrily.

"On'y what I towd him. I said part people went theer o' Sabbath, and that it was a straange niste woshup."

"Nice woshup, indeed! why you niver went theer i' your life," said Sim.

"I said so I'd heerd," said the landlord, stolidly, "and then I towd him how you used to preach theer till they turned thee out."

"What call had you to got to do that?" said Sim, viciously.

"Turned thee out, and took thy name off the plan for comin' to see me."

"Well, of all the unneighbourly things as iver I heerd!" exclaimed Sim. "To go and talk that clat to a straanger."

"Outer kindness to him," said the landlord. "It was a kind o' hint, and he took it, for I was thinking of his bishop, and he took it direckly, for he says, says he, 'Well, I hope I shan't hev my name took off my plan for coming to see you, Mr. Robinson,' he says. 'I hope not, sir,' I says. 'Perhaps you'll take a glass o' wine, sir,' I says. 'No, Mr. Robinson,' he says, 'I'll take a glass—gill you call it—o' your ale.' And if he didn't sit wi' me for a good hour, and drink three gills o' ale and smoke three pipes wi' me, same as you might, ony he talked more sensible."

"Well, he's a pretty parson, he is," sneered Sim.

"You let him be; he aint a bad sort at all," said the landlord, quietly.

"Ha, ha!" laughed Sim. "He's got howlt o' you too, Robinson."

"Mebbe he hev; mebbe he hevn't," said the landlord.

"Did he ask you to go to church?"

"Well, not azackly," said the landlord; "but he said he should be very happy to see me theer, just like astin' me to his house."

"Ho, ho!" laughed Sim; "and some day we shall have the Bull and Cowcumber at church."

"What are yow laughin' at, yo' maulkin?" cried the landlord. "Why, I'd go onywheer to sit and listen to a sensible man talk."

"Aw raight, aw raight, Robinson; don't be put out," said Sim; "but I didn't think as yow'd be got over so easy."

"Who's got over?" said the landlord. "Not I indeed."

"Well," said Sim, "did he say anything more?"

"Say? yes, he's full o' say, and it's good sorter say. I ast him if he'd like to see the farm, and he said he would, and I took him out wheer the missus was busy wi' her pancheons, making bread and syling the milk, and he stopped and talked to her."

"But yow didn't take him out into your moocky owd crewyard, did yo'?"

"Moocky crewyard indeed! but I just did, and I tell you what, Sim Slee, he's as good a judge of a beast as iver I see."

"And then yow showed him the new mare," said Sim, with a grin.

"I did," said the landlord. "'Horncastle?' he says, going up to her and opening her mouth. 'Raight,' I says. 'Six year owd,' he says; and then he felt her legs and said he should like to see her paces, and I had Jemmy to give her a run in the field. 'She's Irish,' he says. 'How do you know?' I says—trying him like to trap him. 'By that turn-up nose,' he says, 'and that wild saucy look about the eye and head.' 'You're raight, parson,' I says. And then he says, 'she was worth sixty pun, every pun of it;' and I told him as I got her for nine and thirty, and ten shillings back. I tell you what, Sim Slee,—Parson's a man, every inch on him. As for the missus, she's that pleased, she sent him ower a pun o' boother this morning from our best Alderney."

"O' course," sneered Sim. "That's the way. That's your cunning priest coming into your house to lead silly women captive, and sew pillows to their armholes."

"Go on wi' yer blather," cried the landlord.

"Go on, indeed," continued Sim. "That's their way. He's a regular Jesooit, he is, and your home wean't soon be your own. He's gettin' ivery woman in the place under his thumb. He begins wi' Miss Eve theer at the house, and Daisy Banks. Then he's gotten howd o' my missus. Here's Mrs. Glaire allus coming and fetching him out wi' her in the pony shay, and now he's gotten howd o' your owd woman, and she's sendin' him pounds o' boother. It was allus the way wi' them cunning priests : they allus get over the women, and then they do what they like wi' the men. No matter how strong they are, down they come just like Samson did wi' Delilah. It was allus so, and as it was in the beginning is now and ever shall be world without end."

"Amen," said Jacky Budd, coming in at the back door. "Gie's a gill o' ale, Robinson. I'm 'bout bunt up wi' thirst. Hallo, Slee, what ! are yow preaching agen ?"

"Never mind," said Sim, sulkily. "I

should ha' thowt parson would ha' fun you in ale, now."

"Not he," said Jacky. "Drinks it all his sen. He's got a little barrel o' Robinson's best i' the house, too."

"Ho, ho, ho!" laughed Sim, holding his sides and stooping. "I say, Jacky, put some new basses in one o' the pews for Mester Robinson, Esquire, as is going to come reg'lar to church now. That's the way they do it: 'Send me in a small barrel o' your best ale, Mr. Robinson,' he says, 'and I shall be happy to see you at church.'"

"If yow use up all yer wind, Sim Slee," said the landlord, sturdily, "yow wean't hev none left to lay down the law wi' at the meeting to-night."

CHAPTER XVII.

MRS. GLAIRE MAKES PLANS.

POOR Mrs. Glaire was in trouble about her fowls, who seemed possessed of a great deal of nature strongly resembling the human. She had a fine collection of noble-looking young Brahma cockerels, great massive fellows, youthful, innocent, sheepish, and stupid. They were intended for exhibition, and their mistress expected a prize for the birds, which had dwelt together in unity, increasing in bulk and brilliancy of plumage, and had never looked a hen in the face since the day they forsook their mamma in the coop.

And now, by mishap, a wanton young pullet had flown up on to the wall that divided them from the poultry yard, and just cried, "Took

— took — took !" before flying down. That
was sufficient: a battle royal began amongst
the brothers directly, and when Mrs. Glaire
went down to feed them she found two birds
nearly dead, the rest all ragged as to their
feathers, bleeding as to their combs and wattles,
and still fighting in a heavy lumbering way,
but so weary that they could only take hold of
one another with their beaks and give feeble
pecks at their dripping feathers.

Mrs. Glaire sighed and made comparisons
between Daisy Banks and the wicked little
pullet who had caused all this strife, telling
herself that she was to be congratulated on
having but one son, and wishing that he were
married, settled, and happy.

She had decided that she would have the
vicar up to dinner that night, and intended to
make him her confidant and ally ; and accord-
ingly in the evening, while the conversation
narrated in the last chapter was going on, the
object of it was making his way to the house,

getting a friendly nod here and there, and stopping for a minute's chat with the people whose acquaintance he had made.

As a rule they were moody faces he met with amongst the women, for they were more than usually soured at the present time on account of the strike, and the sight of the black coat and white tie was not a pleasant one to them, and the replies to his salute were generally sulky and constrained.

He fared better with the men, in spite of Mr. Simeon Slee's utterances, for the report had gone round and round again that Parson could fight, and the church militant, from this point of view, was one that seemed to them worthy of respect.

So he went slowly along the main street, past Mr. Purley, the doctor's, as that gentleman, just returned from a round, was unwedging himself from his gig.

" How do, parson, how do ? " he said. " Like a ride with me to-morrow ? "

"Well, yes, if you'll get out your four-wheeler," said the vicar, laughing.

"Going up to the house to dinner, parson?"

"Yes."

"Tell Mrs. Glaire I'll be on in ten minutes," said the doctor. "But I say, parson, don't sit on the rubber of whist."

"Doctor," said the vicar, patting him on the shoulder, "I shall not; but bring an extra sovereign or two with you, for I want to win a little money to-night for some of my poor."

"He's a rum one," muttered the doctor, as he went in. "He's a rum one, that he is; but I don't think he's bad at bottom."

Meanwhile the vicar went on, past Ramson and Tomson's, the grocers and drapers, where silks and sugars, taffetas and tea were displayed in close proximity; and although Ramson and Tomson were deacons at the Independent Chapel, and the old vicar had passed them always without a look, a friendly nod was exchanged now, to the great disgust of Miss

Primgeon, the lawyer's maiden sister, a lady who passed her time at her window, and who, not being asked to the little dinner she knew was to be held at the house, was in anything but the best of tempers that evening.

Richard Glaire was not aware of his mother's arrangement, and his face wore anything but a pleasant expression as he confronted the vicar in the hall, having himself only just come in.

"How do, Mr. Selwood, how do?" he said haughtily, as he took out his watch and paid no heed to the extended hand. "Just going to dinner; would you mind calling again?"

"Not in the least," said the vicar, smiling, "often. Look here, Richard Glaire," he continued, laying his hand upon the young man's shoulder, "you don't understand me."

"Will you—er—have the goodness——"

"Oh, yes, of course," said the vicar, "I'll explain all in good time; but look here, my good young friend, I'm here in a particular position, and I mean to be a sort of shadow or fate to you."

"I really am at a loss to understand," began Richard, whose anger was vainly struggling against the strong will opposed to him.

"I see," said the vicar, "you've been out and didn't know I was coming to dinner. Don't apologize. Ah, Miss Pelly!"

This to Eve, who had heard the voices; and Richard's face grew white with passion as he saw the girl's bright animated countenance and glad reception of their visitor. She tripped down the stairs, and placed both her hands in his, exclaiming—

"I'm so glad, Mr. Selwood. Aunt didn't tell me you were coming to dinner till just now."

"And so am I glad," he said, with a smile touched with sadness overspreading his face, as he saw the eager pleasant look that greeted him, one that he was well enough read in the human countenance to see had nothing in it but the hearty friendly welcome of an ingenuous maiden, who knew and liked him for his depth and conversation. "We shall have a long chat to-night, I hope, and some music."

They were entering the drawing-room together as he spoke.

"Oh yes, yes," cried she, eagerly. "I can never get Dick to sing now. Do you sing, Mr. Selwood?"

"Well, yes, a little," he said, smiling down at her.

"And play?"

"Yes, a little."

"What? Not the piano?"

"Just a little," he said. "I am better on the organ."

"Oh, I am so glad," cried Eve. "Aunt will be here directly; I'm so glad you've come to Dumford. The old vicar was so stiff, and would sit here when he did come, and play backgammon all the evening without speaking."

"Backgammon, eh?" said the visitor; "not a very lively game for the lookers on."

"Yes, and it was so funny," laughed Eve, "he never would allow cards in his presence, though he played with the dice; and it used to make dear Dick so cross because aunt used to hide the cards. But, oh dear," she exclaimed, colouring slightly, "I hope you don't object to whist."

"My dear Miss Pelly," he said, laughing, "I like every innocent game. I think they all are as medicine to correct the acidity and bitterness of some of the hard work of life."

"Then you'll play croquet with us?"

"That I will."

"Oh, I am glad," cried Eve, with almost childish pleasure. "I can beat Dick easily now, Mr. Selwood, for he neglects his croquet horribly. Mind I don't beat you."

"I won't murmur," he said, laughing.

"But where's aunt?" cried Eve. "She came down before me."

"Aunt" had gone straight into the dining-room to see that all things were in a proper state of preparation, and had stopped short in the doorway on seeing Eve's reception of their guest.

She was about to step forward, when, unseen by him, she caught a glimpse of her son's countenance, as he watched the vicar. His teeth were set, his lips drawn slightly back, and a fierce look of anger puckered his forehead, as with fists clenched he made an involuntary movement after the couple who had entered the drawing-room.

Mrs. Glaire drew back softly, and laying her hand on her beating heart, she walked to the other end of the dining-room, seating herself in one of the windows, half concealed by the curtain.

There was a smile upon her face, for, quick as lightning, a thought had flashed across her mind.

Here was the means at hand to bring her

son to his senses. She had meant to take the vicar into her confidence, and ask his aid, stranger though he was, for she felt that his position warranted it; but now things had shaped themselves so that he was thoroughly playing into her hands.

She knew Eve, that she was ingenuous and truthful, and looked upon her marriage with her cousin as a matter of course. She was a girl who would consider a flirtation to be a crime towards the man who loved her; but the vicar would evidently be very attentive even as he had begun to be, and already Richard's ire was aroused. Richard jealous, she meditated, and he would be roused from his apathetic behaviour to Eve, and all would come right.

"And the vicar?" she asked herself.

Oh, he meant nothing, would mean nothing. He knew the relations of Richard and his cousin, and the plan would—must succeed.

But was she wrong? Was Richard annoyed

at the vicar's demeanour towards Eve, or was it her imagination?

The answer came directly, for Richard flung into the room, took up a sherry decanter, and filling a glass, tossed it off.

"Curse him! I won't have him here," he said aloud. "What does he mean by talking to me like that? by hanging after Eve? I won't have it. You there, mother?"

"Yes, my son," she replied, rising and looking him calmly in the face.

"Look here, mother, I won't have that clerical cad here. What do you mean by asking him to dinner?"

"I asked him as a guest who has behaved very kindly to us, Richard. He is my guest. I asked him because I wished to have him; and you must recollect that he is a clergyman and a gentleman."

"If he wasn't a parson," cried Richard, writhing beneath his mother's clear cold glance, for it seemed to his guilty conscience that she could read in his face that he had broken his word about Daisy—"if he wasn't a parson I'd break his neck."

"Richard, I insist," cried his mother, in a tone that he had not heard since he had grown to manhood, and which reminded him of the days when he was sternly forced to obey, "if you insult Mr. Selwood, you insult your mother."

"But the cad's making play after Eve—he's smiling and squeezing her hand, and the little jilt likes it."

"No wonder," said Mrs. Glaire, calmly. "Women like attentions. You have neglected the poor girl disgracefully."

"What! are you going to allow it?" cried Richard. "I tell you he's making play for her."

"I shall not interfere," said Mrs. Glaire, coldly. "I think Eve ought to have a good husband."

"But she's engaged to me!" half-shrieked Richard.

"Well," said his mother, coldly, though her heart was beating fast, "you are a man, and should counteract it. This is England, and in English society, little as I have seen of it, I know that engaged girls are not prisoners. They are, to a certain extent, free."

"I'll soon stop it," cried Richard, fiercely.

"Stop it then, my son, but mind this : I insist upon proper respect being paid to Mr. Selwood."

"I will," cried Richard, speaking in a deep-pitched voice. "I'll do something."

"Then I should take care that my pretensions to her hand were well known," said Mrs. Glaire, with a peculiar look.

"Pretensions — her hand !" said Richard, with a sneer. "Are you mad, mother, that you take this tone ? I will soon let them see. I'm not going to be played with."

He was about leaving the room, when his mother laid her hand upon his arm.

"Stop, Richard," she said, firmly. "Recollect this—"

"Well, what?"

"That it was the dear wish of your father and myself to make you a gentleman."

"Well, I am a gentleman," cried Richard, angrily.

"Bear it in mind then, my son; and remember that rude, rough ways disgust Eve, and injure your cause. Mr. Selwood is a gentleman, and you must meet him as a gentleman."

"I don't know what you mean, mother," cried the young man, angrily.

"I mean this, that my son occupies the position of the first man in Dumford; and though his father was a poor workman, and his mother a workman's daughter——"

"There, don't always get flinging my birth in my teeth, mother—do, pray, sink the shop."

"I have no wish to remind you of your origin, Richard," said Mrs. Glaire, with a sigh; "only I wish to make you remember that we educated you to be a gentleman, and that we have given you the means.   Act like one."

" I shall do that; don't you be afraid," said Richard.

" And mind, Richard, a true gentleman keeps his word," said Mrs. Glaire, meaningly.

" Well, so do I," exclaimed the young man, flushing up.   " What are you hinting at now?"

" I hope you do, my son; I hope you do," said Mrs. Glaire, looking at him fixedly; and then, as a sharp knock came at the front door, she glided out of the room, and her voice was heard directly after in conversation with the bluff doctor.

" Oh, he's here, too, is he?" muttered Dick, biting his nails.   " Hang it all!   Curse it, how crookedly things go.   I—there, hang it all!"

He stood, thinking, with knitted brows, and then hastily pouring out and tossing off another glass of sherry, and smiling in a way that looked very much like the twitch of the lip when a cur means to bite, he said, in a mock melodramatic voice—

"Ha—ha! we must dissemble!" and strode out of the room.

CHAPTER XVIII.

THE PLAN BEGINS TO WORK.

THE vicar was standing by the flower-stand talking to Eve, and opening out the calyx of a new orchid, a half faded blossom of which he had picked from the pot to explain some peculiarities of its nature, while Eve, looking bright and interested, drank in his every word.

Mr. Purley was filling out an easy chair, having picked out one without arms for obvious reasons, and he was gossiping away to Mrs. Glaire.

"How do, Purley?" said Richard, with a face as smooth as if nothing had occurred to fret him. "Glad to see you."

"Glad to see you too, Glaire; but you don't say, 'How are you?'"

"Who does to a doctor," laughed Richard. " Why you couldn't be ill if you tried."

" Ha-ha-ha!" laughed Mr. Purley. "Well, if I'm not ill, I'm hungry."

"Always are," said Richard, with a sneer; and then seeing that his retort was a little too pointed, he blunted it by pandering to the stout medico's favourite joke, and adding, "Taken any one for a ride lately?"

" Ha-ha-ha!" laughed the doctor. "That's good! He's getting a regular Joe Miller in kid 'gloves, Mrs. Glaire: that he is. Ha-ha-ha!"

Richard gave a short side nod, for he was already crossing the room to the flower-stand.

"Talking about flowers?" he said, quietly. "That's pretty. I didn't know they'd asked you to dinner, Mr. Selwood, and you must have thought me very gruff."

"Don't name it," said the vicar, frankly; but he was looking into the younger man's eyes in a way that made him turn them aside in a shifty manner, and begin picking nervously at the leaves of a plant as he went on—

"Fact is, don't you know, I'm cross and irritable. When a man's got all his fellows on strike or lock out, it upsets him."

"Yes, Mr. Selwood," interposed Eve, "the poor fellow has been dreadfully worried lately. But it's all going to be right soon, I hope."

"I don't know," said Richard, cavalierly; "they're horribly obstinate."

Mrs. Glaire, who had been watching all this eagerly, while she made an appearance of listening to Mr. Purley's prattle, gave her son a grateful look, to which he replied with a smile and a nod, when a servant entered and announced the dinner.

Richard Glaire's smile and nod turned into a scowl and a twitch on hearing his mother's next words, which were—

"Mr. Selwood, will you take in my niece? Mr. Purley, your arm."

The vicar passed out with Eve, followed by

the doctor and their hostess, leaving Richard to bring up the rear, which he did after snatching up a book and hurling it across the room crash into the flower-stand.

"She's mad," he muttered,—"she's mad;" and then grinding his teeth with rage he followed into the dining-room.

Richard contrived to conceal his annoyance tolerably during the dinner, but his mother saw with secret satisfaction that he was thoroughly piqued by the way in which Eve behaved towards their visitor; and even with the effort he made over himself, he was not quite successful in hiding his vexation; while when they went out afterwards on to the croquet lawn, and the vicar and Eve were partners against him, he gave vent to his feelings by vicious blows at the balls, to the no slight damage of Mrs. Glaire's flowers.

This lady, however, bore the infliction with the greatest equanimity, sitting on a garden seat, knitting, with a calm satisfied smile upon her face even though Eve looked aghast at the mischief that had been done.

Matters did not improve, for Richard, after being, to his great disgust, thoroughly beaten, and having his ball driven into all kinds of out-of-the-way places by his adversaries, found on re-entering the drawing-room that he was to play a very secondary part.

Eve recollected that Mr. Selwood could sing a little, and he sang in a good manly voice several songs, to which she played the accompaniment.

Then Eve had to sing as well, a couple of pretty ballads, in a sweet unaffected voice, and all this time the whist-table was waiting and Richard pretending to keep up a conversation with the doctor, who enjoyed the music and did not miss his whist.

At length the last ballad was finished, tea over, and Richard had made his plans to exclude Eve from the whist-table, when he gnashed his teeth with fury, for his mother said—

"Eve, my dear, why don't you ask Mr. Selwood to try that duet with you?"

"What, the one Richard was practising, aunt?"

"Yes, my dear, that one."

"Oh, no," exclaimed the vicar. "If Mr. Glaire sings I will not take his place. Perhaps he will oblige us by taking his part with you."

"But Dick doesn't know it, Mr. Selwood," said Eve, laughing merrily, "and he's sure to break down. He always does in a song. Do try it."

Dick turned livid with rage, for this was more than he could bear, and, seeing his annoyance, Mr. Selwood pleasantly declined, saying—

"But I have an engagement on; I am to win some money of the doctor here, for my poor people."

"Didn't know it was the correct thing to gamble to win money for charity."

"Oh, I often do," said the vicar, pleasantly. "Now I'll be bound, Mr. Glaire, if I'd asked you for a couple of guineas to distribute, you'd think me a great bore."

"You may depend upon that," said Richard. "I never give in charity."

"But at the same time, you would not much mind if I won that sum from you at whist."

"You'd have to win it first," said Richard, with a sneer.

"Exactly," said the vicar; "and I might lose."

"There, don't talk," said Richard; "let's play. Come along, mamma."

Mrs. Glaire was about to excuse herself, but seeing her son's looks, she thought better of her decision, and to keep peace went up to the table; Eve saying she would look on.

It fell about then that the vicar and Mrs. Glaire were partners, and as sometimes happens, Richard and his partner, the doctor, had the most atrocious of hands almost without exception. This joined to the fact that Mrs. Glaire played with shrewdness, and the vicar admirably, so disgusted Richard that at last he threw down the cards in a pet, vowing he would play no more.

"Well, it is time to leave off, really," said the vicar, glancing at his watch. "Half-past ten."

"Don't forget to give your winnings away in charity, parson," said Richard, in a sneering tone.

"Dick!" whispered Eve, imploringly.

"Hold *your* tongue," was the reply. "I know what I'm saying."

"No fear," said the vicar, good-temperedly, as he was bidding Mrs. Glaire good night; "shall I send you an account? Good night, Miss Pelly. Thanks for a delightful evening. Good night, Mr. Glaire."

He held out his hand, and gave Richard's a grip that made him wince, and then, after a few words in the hall, he was gone, with the doctor for companion.

"Thank goodness!" exclaimed Richard, savagely.

"Why, Dick, dear, how cross you have been," said Eve, while Mrs. Glaire watched the game.

"Cross! Enough to make one," he cried, angrily; and then, mimicking the vicar's manner, "Good night, Miss Pelly. Thanks for a delightful evening."

"Well, I'm sure it was, Dick," said Eve; "only you would be so cross."

"And well I might, when you were flirting in that disgraceful way all the evening."

"Oh, Dick!" exclaimed Eve, reproachfully; and the tears stood in her eyes.

"Well, so you were," he cried, "abominably. If anybody else had been here, they would have said that you were engaged to be married to that cad of a parson, instead of to me."

The tears were falling now as Eve laid her hand upon her cousin's shoulder.

" Dick, dear," she whispered ; " don't talk to me like that ; it hurts me."

" Serve you right," he growled.

" If I have done anything to annoy you to-night, dear, it was done in all innocence. But you don't—you can't mean it."

" Indeed, but I do," he growled, half turning his back.

Mrs. Glaire was sitting with her back to them, and still kept busy over her work.

"I am so sorry, Dick—dear Dick," Eve said, resting her head on the young man's shoulder. " Don't be angry with me, Dick."

" Then promise me you'll never speak to that fellow any more," he said, quickly.

" Dick ! Oh, how can I ? But there, you don't mean it. You are only a little cross with me."

" Cross !" he retorted ; " you've hurt me so to-night that I've been wishing I'd never seen you."

" Oh, Dick !" she exclaimed, as she caught

his hand, and raised it to her lips. "Please forgive me, and believe me, dear Dick, that I have not a single thought that is not yours. Please forgive me."

"There, hold your tongue," he said, shortly; "she's looking."

Poor little Eve turned away to hide and dry her tears, and then Mrs. Glaire, looking quite calm and satisfied with the prospect of events, said—

"Eve, my child, it is past eleven."

"Yes, aunt, I'm going to bed. Good night. Good night, Richard."

"Good night," he said, sulkily; and he bent down his head and brushed the candid white forehead offered to him with his lips, while, his hands being in his pockets, he at the same time crackled between his fingers a little note that he had written to Daisy, appointing their next interview, this arrangement having been forgotten in the hurry of the day's parting. And as he spoke he was turning over in his mind how he could manage to get the note delivered unseen by Banks or his wife, for so far as he could tell at the moment, he had not a messenger he could trust.

END OF VOL. I.

www.ingramcontent.com/pod-product-compliance
Lightning Source LLC
Chambersburg PA
CBHW020851020726
47497CB00005B/1357